THE BEAUTIFUL WISHES OF UGLY MEN

THE BEAUTIFUL WISHES OF UGLY MEN

—Stories—

Adam Prince

Black Lawrence Press
New York

Black Lawrence Press
www.blacklawrence.com

Executive Editor: Diane Goettel
Cover Design: Steven Seighman
Interior Design: Rebecca Maslen
Author Photo: John Black Photography

Black Lawrence Press
8405 Bay Parkway C8
Brooklyn, N.Y. 11214
U.S.A.

Published 2012 by Black Lawrence Press, an imprint of Dzanc Books

Many of these stories were previously published in the following, some in different forms:
"Action Figure" *The Southern Review*
"A. Roolette? A. Roolette?" *Narrative Magazine*—Winner of The Winter 2010 Contest
"Island of the Lost Boys" *Sycamore Review*—Winner of The 2010 Wabash Prize for Fiction
"Six Months in, Another Kind of Undressing" *Monkeybicycle*
"Keener" *LIT*
"Big Wheels for Adults" *Missouri Review*
"Ugly Around Him" *Mid-American Review*
"Tranquility" *Northwest Review*

The epigraph for this collection is from *The Works of Love* by Wright Morris, published by The University of Nebraska Press.

Printed in the United States

To Charlotte—who never thought I was ugly to begin with.

What the world needed, it seemed, was a traveler who would stay right there in the bedroom, or open the door and walk slowly about his own house. Who would sound a note, perhaps, on the piano, raise the blinds on the front-room windows, and walk with a candle into the room where the woman sleeps. A man would recognize this woman, this stranger, as his wife.

—Wright Morris, *The Works of Love*

TABLE OF CONTENTS

Big Wheels for Adults 11

Action Figure 35

No Women Tonight 61

Island of the Lost Boys 63

Tranquility 93

Six Months in, Another Kind of Undressing 119

Ugly Around Him 121

Keener 139

Bruises and Baby Teeth 161

Kink 185

A. Roolette? A. Roolette? 189

BIG WHEELS FOR ADULTS

TIME PASSED, AND Peter didn't know what to do. He'd never liked long hugs, not even from women, and this was soon becoming one of the longest of his life. He was getting squirmy, uncomfortable, while Jocko just kept hanging on, pulling so tight that Peter could feel the density of his old friend's fat. It was maybe a full minute before Jocko let out what seemed a conclusive sigh. Peter started to loosen his arms. But Jocko went in for one more clinch. It was to make some point, thought Peter, some claim about who was the better friend, the better man. And though he'd never examined precisely why he didn't like long hugs, a reason appeared to him now: There was something coercive about them.

"I've been doing great," said Jocko, though he didn't look it and Peter hadn't asked. His eyes had gone wider and he'd put on more weight; his skin had the tint of a yellow crayon. He was thirty-one but might have passed for forty-five. Peter felt sorry for his childhood friend and at the same time proud of himself for having gotten through his own thirty-one years looking so much better.

Carli joined them in the entryway, and Jocko bent to kiss her hand. "Lovely to see you," he said, and then in a completely different tone, as if Peter's girlfriend had gone from a princess one moment to a cocktail waitress the next, "How about you make us some Jack and Cokes?"

Carli played along. Made the drinks. Peter smirked to himself, knowing that most women with her education and career would probably have told Jocko to eat shit. But she had never been that way. Unlike Jocko, she seemed to have nothing at all to prove.

Soon the three sat together in Peter and Carli's catalogue-looking living room with its celery and azure color scheme. She had put the room—the entire apartment—together and paid for most of it, too. It was the first nice apartment they'd ever occupied. Peter was cozy there and restless within that coziness, much the way he would get in the midst of a long hug.

Jocko talked and Carli humored him. He told her about the seven thousand dollars he'd just made selling a guitar he'd bought at a pawnshop back when he was on the road. He snapped the cash out of his gold Harley Davidson money clip. "That's a lot of money, huh?" he prompted, and Carli agreed that it was.

Peter knew that Carli was avoiding his glance so as not to give herself—her amusement—away. And this made Peter want to catch that glance all the more. Still, even as he tried, he knew it wouldn't happen. So he looked on with a mix of tenderness and quiet hilarity, the joy of being on the inside of a joke. It was when other people were around that Peter loved her best, and these moments often fueled him through the others.

Not until after Peter had kissed her goodbye did Carli finally relent and look at him. It was a couples' kind of look. An arch in one eyebrow, a private smile communicating how, when he got home tonight, the two of them would review his entire evening, would say to each other, "Can you *believe* that guy?" and agree that no, they could not.

THE LAST TIME Peter had been to a strip club was with Carli on a winter break trip to Montreal back when they were still in college. It was an all-nude place where the women were beautiful in that French way: full lips, easy slenderness, a naked, liquid prowl. And then there was Carli, short and rounded in her puffy orange sweater. They had taken a table far from the stage, Peter facing it and Carli across from him, so that he had to look over her shoulder to see.

While all the other patrons were either catcalling or stewing in a quiet, lustful daze, Peter and Carli had an academic discussion about how, in a strip club, things like power and sincerity were hard to gauge. "It's not the whole objectification thing that bugs me," said Carli, while a dark-skinned blond poured oil down her breasts and stomach. "Or I mean it is, but that's too boring to bring up. It's more this falseness." She pointed out a girl all in pink: high heels, garters, very short skirt. A young girl with her ear to the mouth of a shriveled old man. Her head bobbed along in sympathy to whatever he was telling her. Carli felt bad for the girls, she said, since play-acting along to male fantasy didn't allow room for who they were. Peter tried to see Carli's point and made a counterpoint about how every job involved some acting, whether it was selling real estate or being a U.N. ambassador. It wasn't much of a discussion, really, more a verbal fidgeting, a way of insisting on the world of ideas when the world of things pressed in too hard. Peter couldn't stop staring at the girls, couldn't manage to pull what he knew was a wide, shit-eating grin down off his face.

"But don't you feel sorry for them?" Carli asked, sounding pitiable herself.

"Yeah," he said, but knew it wasn't convincing. And how could it have been coming through that grin? They went on talking—about how much or little money the strippers probably made and about the possible evolutionary impetus behind the appeal of a woman's legs spread wide. But Peter's grin and stare would not leave him, even though he knew Carli was getting even more uncomfortable, her eyes flitting around the room for somewhere safe to look: from the girls, to Peter's face, to the black wall behind him, and down into her plastic cup of lousy red wine.

It had been Carli's idea to go there. She'd been a virgin until Peter, and the first time they'd had sex was just the night before.

Now, looking back, all Peter could guess was that by going to the strip club, Carli had wanted to show how easygoing she could be, how game, and the whole thing just turned out harder than she had imagined.

The two of them walked back to their motel through a light, persistent snow. Peter took off both their clothes and made love to her in the dark. Now, years later, Peter could remember the exact mood of it, a touched and poignant sadness, a need to make everything up to her. And in her own attempt at a conciliatory gesture, Carli had imitated the strippers in the wide way she spread her legs—her thicker, more ordinary legs.

HOPE WAS THIS one's name. All trim curves and youth. A wide-eyed pixie with a mess of dark hair. Braless and perfect in a thin white t-shirt and what seemed to be men's underwear but baby blue with a decal on the front that said, "No Dice" accompanied by a picture of two dice. She wasn't a very good dancer: too routine, and from that bored, half-there look on her face, she might as well have been stirring her morning oatmeal. Still, she was one of the best-looking women Peter had ever seen in real life, and the curve of her waist flaring to hips gave him an instant and painful erection.

He wanted to get lost in the wanting, to fix the whole of his recently preoccupied attention onto the way she was finally, mercifully peeling off that shirt, but Jocko wouldn't shut up.

"Whole lot of options on the table," he was saying. "I got an offer from this producer buddy of mine, Bill Boyd, to manage the Steppenwolf reunion tour. You remember Steppenwolf? 'Born to Be Wild'? Hell yeah, I was. Sober three years and it bore the shit out of me. So the Steppenwolf thing, but then I've got all these ideas, too, this stuff I'm working on. Like Big Wheels for adults. Bigger Big Wheels cause they're for adults. Wait till Crystal gets here. You'll love her. Smoking body and she's got this clit ring . . . I haven't fucked her yet, y'know, because when I'm in a relationship I'm *in* it, but now, you know, *now* . . ." He slapped the table, waved around his beer.

Jocko and his girlfriend had just broken up, so this was a night of proving that he was better off without her. He often had dramatic breakups, but what made this one particularly hard for him was the fact that his now ex-girlfriend was Simone White, the famous folk singer, and over the year or so he'd been with her, Jocko had started thinking of himself as famous by association. Simone had even made him her tour manager, despite the fact that his work experience up to that point had been limited to odd jobs in the service industry, selling coke, transporting coke across the Mexican border, and laying tile with a company connected to his rehab. So now Jocko was out of a job too and putting money he probably couldn't afford to lose into strippers' underwear.

"Hey, Pete," he continued as Hope crawled by with her t-shirt in her teeth, "did I tell you I've got this whole other name?

Yeah. I'm really someone else, man. Kyle Windward. My real mom's part Chippewa Indian. I found out all about her. I could stalk her or whatever. God, Pete, you wouldn't believe all the pussy I got back when I was dealing. I'd show up at a chick's apartment and maybe she wouldn't have all the money, so, y'know, what I'd do is . . ."

And Peter almost said it. Almost interrupted with, "Listen, Carli's pregnant." Not because he wanted Jocko to know, but because he wanted Jocko to stop talking, and this was the only thing he could think of. He put that thought down and grabbed another. "So what happened with Simone, anyway?" he asked. "What's the story?"

Jocko took a swig of beer and looked into the middle distance between Hope's legs. "We're just on different paths right now," he said. And Peter knew that this was the only explanation he was going to get.

MORE GIRLS STARTED to arrive. They came in jeans and t-shirts, then into the women's bathroom and out again in white lingerie, in pigtails, in nighties and knee socks, in cheerleader outfits, in panties made of fine, shiny chains.

Peter was reminded of a night when, flipping channels, he had lingered on a women's wrestling match between a nurse and a schoolgirl. Carli was surprised he could be interested in such a cliché, and Peter had explained to her—only realizing the truth of it as he spoke—that when it came to lust, a thing like cliché didn't matter. Because lust was a region into which the critical mind could only get so far. You could talk evolutionary psychology; you could talk feminism or Freud or the way it should be, but those were only dirt roads into lust, and sometime in the night, they would be washed away.

A woman with blond dreadlocks high heeled her way over to them. Older than most of the others with a loose beer gut, she was so far off from Jocko's description of Crystal that Peter didn't know who she was until the second time Jocko had said her name.

This discrepancy was gratifying to Peter. He didn't actually see Jocko all that often, but Carli and he tended to talk about his old friend a lot. Offering people they knew up for discussion was a hobby of theirs, and with Jocko there was just so much to discuss. There was the time they'd run into him at a coffee shop and he claimed to having found the cure for cancer, which apparently involved crossbreeding pot with some kind of wild rose. There was the time a few Christmases back when Jocko's mom was at Peter's parents' house to show off her new pure breed, and she said to Peter matter-of-factly, "Our son didn't work out for us, so now we have a dog." And then, of course, there was the Simone White story, a favorite among Peter and Carli's friends for months. At dinner parties, they would offer it up, uncover it like a steaming, buttery lobster dish. Most of their friends wanted to talk about how this could possibly have happened, how the woman who'd written love songs like "Even Call" and "A History of Somewhere Else" could possibly go for someone like Jocko even if he *was* twenty years younger than she. But what interested Peter most in these conversations was how Jocko challenged the norm of how to live a life. Granted, Peter would say, the man was a mess—unstable, ill-equipped for happiness, likely to die any day from an overdose or a gun to the head—but then this same restlessness had also led to moments of extreme vitality and a sort of grace that had allowed Jocko to live in a mansion in Mendocino, have orgies, go hang-gliding in Yellowstone Park, and become Simone White's boyfriend, if only for a year. It was a question, Peter would insist, of high highs and low lows versus stability. And though he had made this same argument half a dozen times, whenever he was actually with Jocko, Peter found himself looking for counterevidence: that maybe the highs weren't really all that high or else the lows too low to make them worth it. If Crystal wasn't anything close to the way she'd been described, then maybe the hang-gliding and orgies weren't either.

Jocko bought the three of them shots of whiskey with beer chasers and now he was telling Crystal about Peter and their childhood friendship. Smash ball, butts up, sneaking into Stephen Pickney's house to watch their first porno. In Peter's opinion, it wasn't anything all that interesting for someone who hadn't lived it, but either Crystal was interested after all or great at faking it.

"You see this guy?" Jocko said, lobbing an arm around Peter. "We've known each other since we were *one*."

Another favorite topic between Peter and Carli was why he bothered with Jocko at all. She never asked the question in a mean way. It was just that she wanted to know. Really, it was a good question, a question with any number of answers and none of them quite sufficient. Peter might say, for instance, that it was a vicarious thrill, that since he himself had never done heroin or lived in the streets or killed a kitten by accidentally slamming a door on it during a fight with a girlfriend, he wanted to know what all that was like. Or else he might talk about lingering guilt brought on by the fact that he'd had a stable upbringing while two blocks down in a house even nicer than his, Jocko's adopted dad was telling him what a constant letdown he was and his adopted mom was ignoring him. Or maybe this renewed, false friendship was a tribute to that real friendship of their youth, a friendship that had run as deep as human relationships do, deeper in many ways than Peter's relationship with Carli, even if he couldn't now say why and had lost the whole timbre of it somehow in the process of growing up. But then, Peter had never been good with feelings, had never trusted them or quite understood what they were. Or else maybe he had. Maybe he used to and just didn't anymore.

Jocko had gone off for a lap dance with Crystal. Peter was trying to wave Hope down for a lap dance of his own and thinking all these things about Jocko as a way of distracting himself from

Carli's pregnancy.

The girls were starting to repeat on stage and it was comforting to Peter how much less interesting they were this second time around. He ordered another beer, started to feel good, relaxed, ready to go home. He'd had his bit of wildness for the night and he would return to Carli and report back: Jocko is lost, his life a fantasy, let us now proceed with ours.

Somewhere in the middle of Peter's resolve, Jocko had returned. He was saying something into Peter's ear, and it took awhile to register what it was. He was going to get the two of them invited over to Crystal's house along with Hope.

"Jocko . . ." Peter began, but he was cut off.

"What?" said Jocko. "Just hanging out and then whatever you decide, okay?" He took a long swig of beer and swished it around in his mouth while shaking his head. Then he said, "Pete Rickersly: doing the right thing," as if it were an ad on a sign.

IT WAS JUST last week that Carli had told Peter about the pregnancy. She'd taken him out for steaks at Pacific Dining Car, his favorite place.

Peter's first reaction was relief. In all the time he'd been with her, he couldn't decide whether or not to get married, and now the decision was made for him. He imagined himself the good husband, going to Lamaze classes, chasing down hoagies with extra pickles at midnight. But as they continued to talk and Carli kept saying things like, "We can do anything we want to about this, okay?" Peter understood that the decision wasn't made for him at all, that Carli was asking him to make it, putting him in charge the same way she'd insist on going to the restaurant he wanted to go to, renting the movie he wanted to rent. Peter made a short, angry laugh. She'd always been that way: so maddeningly accommodating, so undemanding that he was always made the villain. His fantasy of being a good husband shifted then to a fantasy of undressing their young, white-bloused waitress in the waiting area between bathrooms: He would pop those buttons loose. Except that he wouldn't. Wouldn't ever, because Carli was pregnant.

As the conversation went on, Peter began to describe the pregnancy as "tricky" and "complicated." He pointed out that Carli had just started her new job, and he wondered aloud whether this was the right time. In the end then, they'd come to no decision, and the topic had been laid aside.

WHAT PETER WAS going to say before Jocko had cut him off was that maybe getting invited to Crystal's house wasn't as easily arranged as Jocko seemed to think, since a false display of interest was basically a stripper's job. And now as they sat on a curb by the back door of the club, it was becoming increasingly evident that Peter's doubt was justified.

Most of the other girls had already left. They exited

wearing their street clothes, and often without make-up. They looked tired, relieved. The bouncers escorted them out, and the girls would glance at the two men on the curb with suspicion or amusement.

"Takes them awhile to change," said Jocko for the third or fourth time. "They gotta pay out and shit." He was getting nervous, wiggling his knees, and Peter knew that soon this nervousness would slip into anger, that Jocko would throw some kind of fit.

Peter tried to think of something to say, one of those heartfelt things he didn't say unless he was drunk, because then they felt more true. Jocko was always building up expectations, riding people so hard that at some point their letting him down was inevitable. Peter wanted to explain that. He wanted to say that we are all at our most brilliant in the ways we find to suffer, and thus happiness depends on modifying expectations. Look at me, Peter would say. I couldn't get a lap dance with Hope, so I had one with another girl instead, and that was all right because it needed to be. Look at me. I have a girlfriend who isn't unattractive, really, just doesn't exercise or wear tight clothes or flirt with my friends to make me jealous. She has other qualities. Her attraction is in the unexpected things she says, so that at one moment she might be talking about the several interesting connections between the terms "dry hump" and "dry heave" and in the next she will exclaim with absolute earnestness, "God, it's a beautiful day!" But you have to settle, Jocko. You always do. My girlfriend is pregnant, so I need to make a decision soon. And, yes sometimes when I'm out with her and a beautiful woman walks by, it isn't just lust I feel, but rage.

Peter didn't get a chance to deliver his speech, though, because as he was concocting it, Crystal and Hope emerged from the back door of the club and came toward them across the lot with a couple of finger-wiggling waves hello.

So maybe this was another reason why Peter still went out with Jocko sometimes: Jocko pulled him into things.

WITH CRYSTAL'S MEDICINE cabinet open and facing the other bathroom mirror, Peter was able to get a good angle for checking his bald spot. He'd been doing a lot of this lately, trying to determine just how bad it was. He'd noticed that most of his balding friends were married and most of his friends with full heads of hair still single, and he had several pet theories about this, but he himself was somewhere between. He would often ask Carli about the bald spot, and she kept assuring him it was barely noticeable, but then she had a tendency to put kindness before truth. All the same, his hair looked good tonight. So Peter pushed Carli back out of his mind and exited the bathroom feeling confident.

"Where's Bill Boyd?" Crystal was asking. "When's Bill Boyd gonna get here?" She was a songwriter, and it turned out that Jocko had managed to get Peter and himself invited here on the promise that Jocko's producer friend was coming see her play. So she'd been scurrying around her little place in The Valley picking Legos and underwear out of the thick green carpet, throwing stuffed animals into one plastic bag and beer cans into another, and explaining that her kid was at his grandma's house. Now she kept running into the bedroom and emerging in different outfits, different versions of herself for Boyd to see. The other three sat around the coffee table talking, doing coke, passing a bottle of Jack Daniels, and watching the TV on mute.

Jocko was saying you always had to use a hundred dollar bill for coke because it was better that way and you always knew you could afford more. Peter, who'd only done it a few times before and never this much was telling Hope that the night was a thing you could tune into like a radio frequency, swim into like the current of a river so you stopped making decisions and just let it carry you along.

Hope had that bored, oatmeal-stirring look on her face. She sat there blowing her beauty all over the room. And it seemed to Peter that beauty itself was the problem. Beauty that made him restless with Carli, beauty that had made Hope bored and detached and tired of what men could offer.

Hope was maybe three feet away from him on the couch, and he was as conscious of that distance as he was of the shortness of her shorts, the contours of her thighs, the fact that she wore no bra or make-up and didn't need to. She wriggled her lithe and tidy self over to the edge of the couch, used one hand to hold her hair back and the other to pinch shut one nostril while also maneuvering the rolled bill. And even this potentially awkward movement was fluid. Assured.

Peter's phone rang. It was Carli. Just checking in, she'd probably say, calling to see if he was all right. Peter didn't answer. He shut off the phone and leaned over to take his turn with the coke.

On the TV was one of those late-night cable sex comedies with all the actual sex cut out. The tan kid who washed people's yachts only had to take off his shirt and he would have spring break girls and trophy wives all over him.

Crystal appeared in a forties dress, then an executive a-line, then a silver miniskirt.

The two men were talking about the way Jocko used to fight, how tough he'd been. Peter pointed out that Jocko never started with a lot of pushing like the rest of the kids did, but he'd put his hands behind his back, lean in close to the other kid and say something quiet, something like "is there going to be a problem here?" as if he'd decided to be diplomatic. "But then," Peter continued, "then he'd just whip his fists around to destroy the kid." The two of them recounted fights with Lance Kennedy, Ely Macgregor, Darren Norton. They spoke, Peter guessed, for the women's benefit, though he'd never actually met a woman who seemed impressed by fighting.

Crystal finally decided on a hippy skirt and a lot of makeup that was supposed to make her look younger but only made her look older for trying.

Hope drifted into the kitchen for a beer, and Jocko followed. The kitchen was partitioned off from the living room with a bar. Peter could see Jocko nudge up close to Hope, see the two of them whispering.

When she returned to the couch, Hope took off her shoes and lay back lengthwise, so that her toes were two inches from Peter's left thigh.

Jocko was pulling Crystal into the bedroom. She asked about Boyd again.

"Will you shut up about that?" Jocko told her. "Will you have some manners?" It was said playfully, but there was menace behind it. The bedroom door clicked shut.

"More coke," Hope announced, and she went to work assembling lines. The tan kid in the TV movie had fallen into the water, and a cuckolded husband was trying to run him down with a racing boat while the wife fought for control of the wheel.

"Pete, could you hold back my hair?" asked Hope. Peter grabbed a fistful. It gave off a scent of cinnamon and talcum. Her shirt rode up as she dipped to the table, and he could see the back of that baby blue No Dice underwear. Meanwhile, on the TV, a shark had appeared. And seeing the shark, the cuckolded husband drove off, leaving the tan kid to his fate. Then a commercial break.

"Here," said Hope handing over the rolled bill. "I made that other line for you. Wasn't that sweet?"

Peter told her it was. When he went in for the coke, she bit him on the side just under his armpit. She giggled and rolled. Peter watched her, wondering what he should do, and—more than that—what he would.

The shark actually turned out to be the tan kid's skinny friend who was wearing a shark fin for some reason Peter couldn't establish. The moral of the movie seemed to be that sex was all in good fun, a thing without real consequences. People got mad about cheating, yes, but their anger only made them silly—figures of comedy.

From behind the bedroom door came moaning. Peter felt himself blush. Hope laughed at him. And when he leaned down for another try at the coke, she bit him again, this time on the back of the neck.

Several thoughts came at Peter as he felt her lips and teeth flush through him. He told himself life was short, and he wondered if Jocko had paid her. He reasoned that if he was going to cheat, it should be with a woman as beautiful as Hope. He tried to look at this as some kind of bachelor party. He decided that he had done the noble thing in loving a woman he was not more attracted to, and he figured he deserved this. He blamed the coke, and then he blamed Carli. Finally, without turning around, he said to Hope, "I have a girlfriend. She's pregnant."

"Oh," said Hope. "Congratulations." She got up and walked outside.

Peter sat a moment on the couch, unsure of what he'd done and why. From behind the bedroom door in gasps came the kind of dirty talk he'd often fantasize about while masturbating but had never felt comfortable actually using himself. He wasn't sure what to do, but eventually followed Hope outside so that he wouldn't have to keep listening.

The girl was perched on the concrete steps smoking a cigarette.

"So, I guess you're the first to know," Peter told her.

"Uh-huh." She took a long drag and then another.

Peter tried to think of something to say. "I left her once," is what came to mind. "About a year ago. I remember crying and kicking the furniture while I got together some clothes. And at the same time she was in the kitchen putting stuff in a paper bag. A bottle of water, a packet of Kleenex, some crackers, my favorite cheese—like a care package for me to take on the drive away from her." He stopped. He breathed. "What do you do with a person like that?" he asked. "I mean, how can you tell someone you love to stand up for herself against you?"

He wasn't sure Hope was listening. But eventually she asked, "You figure she knew you'd come back?"

"I don't know."

"She knew you'd come back," said Hope. "And now," she

said, mashing the cigarette into the concrete, "Well, now I guess you're back."

The two of them sat awhile looking out into the dark nothing of The Valley.

"It's early in the . . ." Peter said. "I mean, it's before the, uh, first trimester. I just. We haven't. She's great. I mean, Carli is. She's great."

Hope had that bored expression on her face again. But maybe it was a little different this time or maybe Peter just saw it differently. A look of disappointment and retreat. A look that said, of course. Of course, the world is like this.

When the two of them got back inside, they saw Jocko and Crystal, shirtless and facing each another in the middle of the living room. She was accusing him, saying Bill Boyd wasn't coming over, wasn't ever going to come over and he'd made it up to get in her pants. Sweat dripped down into a sagging, freckled cleavage as she spit out accusations: "Phony, fucking, liar. Average, fucking, prick."

Jocko stood still, hands behind his back. He droned in a low, cool monologue that drifted in and out of sense. "Come over to your place . . . hook you up . . . buy all that coke . . . cool, cool . . . and Billy Boyd can suck my dick cause I got a whole other name . . ." There was something familiar in that stance, but it took Peter a moment to figure out what: Jocko was going to hit her.

Peter put his hand on Jocko's shoulder, said, "Hey, man, let's get going," with a voice as full of cheer as he could manage.

He was trying to create a mood in which violence would be impossible. And when Jocko turned around toward him, Peter saw on his face the timidity of the kid he used to be, the kid who lived in a house with couches he wasn't allowed to sit on, the kid who couldn't go to sleep at night without listening to audiotapes of a person he'd never met before reading him *Paddington Bear*.

THE CAB RIDE home was quiet. Passing streetlights illuminated Jocko's face between bars of shadow.

The cab stopped at Peter and Carli's first, and Jocko got out for a hug. He started to cry. "I miss her, y'know?" he said of Simone. "I gave her my whole heart and whatever she wanted and then," he choked, "she left me." He gasped and buckled in Peter's arms, heaving with a desperate fury the more stable man found himself envying almost as much as he had the moans of lust half an hour before. "You love me, don't you Pete?" Jocko asked. "You love me?"

"Yeah," said his friend eventually.

"You love me," continued Jocko. "I know you do because you came out with me tonight when I needed you to, because why else would you come?"

"Yeah," said Peter again. "I love you," feeling this time not just the need to agree, but the need to mean it, too. And maybe he almost did.

"ARE YOU ALL right?" asked Carli, the way she always did when Peter came to bed after her. She wasn't awake when she asked it; the question came from somewhere inside her sleep, a concern for Peter that seemed to dominate even her unconscious mind.

Her round cheek was mashed against the pillow, her body, which bore so little resemblance to Hope's, encased in a tight purple teddy. The lingerie was an attempt to make their sex life better, and in some ways it had, but it also drew attention to the fact that their sex life wasn't very good to begin with. It was like that question, *Are you all right?* Even asleep she seemed to be waiting for an answer.

"Yeah," he told her, just as he'd said *yeah* to Jocko only a few minutes before—less a lie than the expression of a wish.

Peter got into bed. He told himself he'd done the right thing in not having sex with Hope and that the reward for a man like himself was a clear conscience and a good night's sleep. Still, he couldn't sleep, kept shifting—uncomfortable in every position.

All that shifting eventually woke up Carli. "How'd it go?" she asked looking sleepy-pleased to see him.

He wanted to tell her everything. Yet he found himself editing certain bits out: the coke, the conversation on the steps with Hope, his own desire. "This other girl," he said. "She kind of threw herself at me. I think Jocko paid her." He forced out a chuckle to indicate how insignificant this other girl had been, how easy to refuse.

And as he spoke, he began to think about the difficulty of accounting for the distance between who a person was and who that person would like to be, between ourselves and the performances we put on for those we hope will love us. There was Jocko and his bravado. Crystal suiting up into different versions of herself in order to prepare for a man she had never met before but was determined to win. There was Peter himself, who'd been performing all night and continued to do so now. And then there was Carli.

He knew she must have suspected there was more to the story than he told her. Still, she didn't bring it up. Instead she asked whether he thought Jocko would have really hit Crystal. Peter said he wasn't sure, and the two of them analyzed Jocko awhile just as they had silently promised each other they would. In the dark of their bedroom, they pitied him, laughed at him. Then came a quiet. The stillness before something happens. With some anxious mix of emotions, Peter waited for Carli to bring up her pregnancy, to express a desire, to say, *this is what I need*, so that he might then do the right thing, be the right man. But time went by and she didn't. Finally, just before falling asleep, she reached over, put her arms around him and said, "It was nice of you to go out with Jocko tonight; he just looks up to you so much,"—which was, Peter realized, exactly what he had wanted to hear.

ACTION FIGURE

"YOUR MOTHER AND I can't talk to you anymore."

"Why not?"

"You know why not."

". . . Okay," says Kid. "I know why not." He hangs up, shuts off his phone, looks into a sky the color of concrete and thinks of all the messages traveling through. All the meanings behind them. In truth, he doesn't know why not. He only has suspicions. It could be because he hacked apart the Thanksgiving turkey to prove a point or because he'd left rehab again, but there are other, less obvious possibilities.

Everything means something, but it's hard knowing what. Two jumpsuit men from the L.A. Department of Water and Power are down in the aqueduct poking their instruments into its trickle of water. They could be engineers or spies. Just like Kid's shitty apartment building next to the aqueduct could be an accusation that he's not what his father had hoped, or else it could be the exact opposite: part of a way to hide his true importance, a disguise so deep that even he isn't sure of it.

Because Kid has seen things he wasn't supposed to have seen. Big-shouldered military men leading collared dog creatures down the aqueduct at midnight. TV channels hidden between other TV channels on which the killing is real. Kid suspects the Department of Water and Power. He's seen the movie *Chinatown* and believes himself a topic of discussion in basements and control rooms, gigantic photos of his face on various screens.

Kid is not a kid. He's thirty-two years old. His real name is Colin Deanford, though the only person who calls him Colin is his father. Or used to be. Now his father calls him "you," as in, "Your mother and I can't talk to you anymore."

BACK INSIDE THE apartment, Kid grips the cell phone in his right hand and a slice of bread in his left.

"Yesterday," says Pamela from the other end of the couch, "I saw these two guys in the exact same suit pass each other right in front of the building."

Kid doesn't answer. He's too busy hating this apartment with the carpet stains and the dead potted plants and the crumpled fast food bags. He's too busy hating freckled, ungrateful her.

"Last night," she says, "I heard these noises from the aqueduct. Like these animal noises. Did you?"

"They can track you," he says. "With your cell phone on, they can track you."

"Who can?"

"What?"

"Who can?"

"I don't know yet."

Something is on the TV. People fighting each other with great, powerful hands, shooting each other to save the world.

"Hey," says Kid, "I need sixty bucks."

"For Bug?"

"Yeah. For Bug."

"I thought it was forty."

"Are you saying you don't believe me? Are you making that accusation?"

Pamela says she's not. She disappears behind the bedroom door, and he hears the lock on her safe click loose. It's *her* safe, even though they live together.

Kid's not hungry. The bread has slipped from his hand and now he's gripping the money instead.

"Eighty total," she tells him. "The extra twenty's for my face stuff. I need you to pick it up." She's squinching that face into this certain expression, this you're-taking-advantage-of-my-car-wreck-money expression she never used to get.

Pamela is only eighteen, but she's already had a baby the courts have taken away and already developed a phobia about going outside. So she depends on Kid. He met her at a bus station, and the first thing she ever said to him was *help*.

The face stuff is to keep her from getting zits.

She says.

TONIGHT THE WALGREENS is empty of customers. It's just employees, maybe ten employees gathered around a single cash register.

"You guys open?" asks Kid taking half a step in the direction of Pamela's face stuff.

"Yeah," says one, an employee with a Santa Claus hat.

"So . . . what are you all doing here?"

"We're waiting for you," says the employee.

Kid backs away and out the sliding door. Once outside, he runs.

His first job had been at a Walgreens, stocking shelves back when he was only fifteen. One time, he'd skipped work and lied to his manager that it was because his father had died. Somehow, his father found out about that.

And then there was Kid's most recent stay in detox, which only happened because his father had tricked him. Kid was mad about the trick, so he said something to the intake guy about plans to have his father murdered. And even though the detox people had promised total confidentiality, his father had found out about that, too.

Kid is beginning to suspect it's all connected, that the reason his father found out and the reason he told Kid he couldn't talk to him anymore is because of the Department of Water and Power. The connection between these two probably started way back at USC medical school, since anybody will tell you that USC is a connection kind of place.

Dr. Deanford became a celebrated surgeon soon after his residency. His hands would enter the insides of senators and holy men. Then the doctor met a pretty college girl who liked to do sculpture in her spare time. He married her and had a son, but this son wasn't Kid. This son was Orion, who drowned in their swimming pool one night when he was two. So Dr. Deanford and his wife decided to adopt, which means that Kid isn't really Kid Deanford or even Colin Deanford, but someone else, with a name unknown even to himself.

Kid understands these facts but not what they mean, just as he understands that some connection must exist between his father and the Department of Water and Power, between the Department of Water and Power and Orion who drowned, between this moment in Walgreens and that moment at a different Walgreens seventeen years before. He's slipping around on information like trying to move through a dumpster full of dead fish.

"I wish I could say I'm surprised," is what his father had said about the murder threats from detox. It was the same thing he'd said about what had happened with the boss at Walgreens, and even a long time before that when Kid had stumbled over Ravel's "Piano Concerto for the Left Hand" after seven years of lessons.

BUG HAS A tiny video camera taped to the peephole of his front door, and his TV displays the view: a dirty courtyard with a dirty swimming pool. No one out there. Nothing happening.

On the couch staring into the screen is Bug's girl Lina. She's pucker-lipped and starving thin, so it's hard to know if she's erotic or disgusting, sort of like Bug's lava lamps and neon 3-D posters that show different things the longer you look. She watches the TV with such attention that Kid starts thinking there might be more to it than he can see.

"You guys were watching me on there," Kid says. "Were you watching me on there?"

"The camera only records," says Bug. "It doesn't transmit."

"What?"

"It's a recording. This happened yesterday."

"But," says Kid, "nothing's happening."

"This was yesterday," says Bug. "If I put in the other memory card and fast-forwarded, we'd see you arrive. We'd see you knocking and waiting, yelling at me to open the door because you've got the twenty you owe me. We can watch it if you want."

But Kid doesn't want to watch himself standing there being nervous at the door and doesn't want to say so, either. So instead he says, "Twenty bucks? You wouldn't let me in because of twenty bucks? Is that all our friendship means to you?" He tries to make his voice sound loud and sure so that Lina will know the difference between him and Bug, what kind of man each is. And as he speaks, he imagines Lina kneeling to suck him off, the way her eyes would widen in lust and admiration, the way his hands would reach down to control her. He raises the money, all eighty dollars, up into the air and slaps it down in Bug's hands to demonstrate how little such things mean to a man like himself.

The meth Bug gets is good, glass grade. But he sells mostly weed and smokes only weed himself, so every time you get meth from him, you get a lecture too. "Look at yourself," Bug says. "Will you look at yourself?"

THE NEXT MORNING Kid shuffles back toward the apartment under a glaring sun. He has no money or face stuff and he's trying not to think about how disappointed Pamela is going to be or how disappointed his father already is. He's trying not to think of how it will soon be Christmas.

On the brown edge of somebody's lawn, Kid sees the action figure. It wears a white suit and its right hand grips a pistol. Kid turns it around in the sun to discover a face that looks like his.

Pamela is asleep when he gets back. He locks himself in the bathroom, crouches next to the cabinet under the sink where the mirror can't see him. He gets out the action figure and the baggie. He smokes. He studies the action figure, looks into its face, its nothing face, an expression between expressions, and he understands that this figure doesn't just look like him. It *is* him somehow. Kid cradles this smaller self in both hands. It's worn down with use and play, so that, in places, the color of plastic skin scuffs through. He has such pity for it. He's crying.

Then he's got a thought but needs a dollar, too. He leaves the bathroom to search under the couch and in the drawer of wires disconnected from the things they were supposed to hook into; he digs among the cigarette butts in the dirt of the dead potted plants, sinks hands into the pockets of Pamela's clothes on the floor.

Once he's got a dollar, he cuts a bit off the corner in the shape of another miniature dollar, which he tapes to the figure's left hand. He stows the figure in the cupboard under the sink behind the drainpipe. The bigger dollar he takes with him.

THE LIQUOR STORE man refuses to accept the dollar because of the cut from the corner. He looks at Kid with eyes that glare accusing as the sun. It's the glare of school administrators and bosses from Walgreens, the shoe store, the Target, the Denny's. It's the glare of the jobs themselves and their uniforms that make a man ordinary. The glare of other liquor store men on other days. Like the day Kid lost his job at Denny's and went to get a forty with change he'd begged only to see his father on the cover of the *Los Angeles Times*. "Wonder Doc Performs First Successful Face Transplant," the headline said. Then the liquor store man said that Kid better buy that paper or put it down, which caused

Kid to scramble over the counter and pound the glare out of him.

But even though the glare is the same, the day is different. Kid knows all about the laws that govern the acceptance of cash and tells the man so. Then he repeats "One lottery ticket, please," perfectly calm, perfectly cheerful, because it's easy to control your rage when you know you're going to win. He scratches the ticket right there and wins two hundred and fifty dollars, the maximum paid in store. "Christmas money," Kid says.

Then he goes to Walgreens for Pamela's face stuff. It's a whole different place this morning and he a whole different Kid.

Afterward, he struts toward home, already comfortable under the sun and certain of what it means: The sun is a spotlight shining down on a man unlike other men, a man able to hold his own fate securely in one hand.

TONIGHT KID AND Pamela are putting the world together. They conclude that there are three levels of the Department of Water and Power: the laborer types who've been in the aqueduct lately and double as spies, the military types with the dog creatures that Pamela may have heard but only Kid has seen, and now the men in identical suits. It all makes so much sense, is coming through so clear. Kid and Pamela are students of meaning and connectivity. The meth helps keep them in this high frequency of wisdom.

"They call it glass," says Kid, "because you can see right

through it. You can see right. Through it."

Pamela laughs. She's looking at him the way she used to, with the admiration he deserves. She's a sweet and pretty girl, a freckled, small-chinned, helpless girl. He tells her about going into the Walgreens last night with all of those employees there, but in this version of the story he doesn't run. "See, I got your face stuff," he says. "You didn't think I would."

"Yeah, I did," says Pamela. "I did."

"No you didn't, but that's okay." He flits a hand through the air to show just how okay it is, how easily he can forgive her. "Kid takes good care of you, doesn't he?"

Pamela agrees. The meth is good. They decide to slam it and now they're nicely spun.

A man on the TV is kissing one person, killing another.

Pamela starts talking about some court thing to get her baby back, and Kid tries to listen but he's spinning out in some other direction.

"That Lina," he says. "Bug's girl. You can tell she's tweaking. All spacey and skinny, but Bug can't see it. Sometimes people can't see things because they don't want to look. Or else they look, but they don't know what things mean. My parents are probably going to want us to come over for Christmas Eve."

"Did they ask you?"

"Not yet, but I think they will."

"Even after what happened?"

"What happened?"

"At Thanksgiving?"

But Kid doesn't want to talk about that. He's decided it isn't important. "All those employees at Walgreens looked familiar," he says. "Like people I've seen in bars or whatever. I think they all work for my dad. Like he hired them to watch me. There's some kind of plan with the Department of Water and Power. They're going to offer me a job, I think. To be one of the guys in suits."

"Really? How do you know?"

But any more information would lead to telling her about the action figure, so he tells her he loves her instead.

SOMETIME LATER, THE next day or the next, Kid cuts off a corner of a twenty, tapes that to the action figure's left hand, then goes to the races and wins six thousand dollars on an exacta. At the mall he buys a new white suit. At the pawnshop he finds a Colt .38 Super pistol that looks almost exactly like the one carried by the figure. The pawnshop man is friendly and respectful, asking for no certificate, no paper work at all, as if Kid is perfectly entitled to buy that gun. As if he is meant to.

So here is Kid's new self in a white suit. Here he is at Bug's apartment, buying half an ounce and handing off a chunk to Lina when Bug's not looking. Here he is at a jewelry store getting a gold bracelet to give Pamela on Christmas Eve. Here in the back room of The Alibi announcing, "Drinks all around, courtesy of Kid!" Here behind the dumpster on the edge of the aqueduct, aiming the pistol at the heads of those two Department of Water and Power men out there with their instruments. He doesn't fire; he's practicing, getting used to the power in his hands.

These days he's tuned into the world and the world behind it. So he's got to stay up to take so much in. No sleep in a week, and his visions come through clear as reality. Agents watching him, evaluating him from the other side of hidden cameras. A whole miniature world of action figures somewhere deep inside the DWP complex—a place where you are played with. There are figures giving speeches, mailing packages, stocking shelves at Walgreens. Figures stabbing other figures in miniature parks and sneaking into parents' bedrooms to steal their mothers' diamond earrings.

A son figure arrives three hours late for Thanksgiving dinner with a girl figure about half his age and looking it. His little cousin figures are there and his aunt figure, too. He's chewing through salad, pretending sobriety. He's got an investment idea that's just going to need a few thousand is all, but his father figure refuses to listen. Then the girl he brought starts talking about her lost baby even though he's warned her not to, warned her that in this family lost babies are not talked about. So, in an attempt to change the subject, the son offers to carve the turkey. His hand grips the special, expensive Japanese knife. "No, not like that," says the father figure, a master carver himself. "Jesus, can't you do anything right?" So the son is angry. His action arm swings down on the turkey, hacking as he yells, "Orion! Orion, Orion, OrionOrionORIONORION!" The pieces chip off, jump into the cranberry sauce and into his mother's lap.

HAVING A GIRLFRIEND who's afraid to go out isn't always as good as it sounds, because it means she's always home. And Pamela goes on these tweak missions of taking things apart. The blender, the clock radio. Kid had a computer once, but now it's only pieces. He had to tape a note on the front of the TV: "Do not take apart." And then there's the snooping, the threat of her finding things. The money. The pistol. The action figure. He told her about winning at the races, but said it was just luck and just five hundred. The pistol he keeps close and she hasn't found it yet. But the action figure is something else. Kid doesn't like the idea of carrying it with him, worries about getting robbed or losing it—but then, it's vulnerable under the bathroom sink, too. He's put his stash in the drawer with the disconnected wires, because she's found it there before. It's a red herring, a decoy to keep her from the figure. He wants her to find it again, break off a little, smoke it, and then stop snooping.

Still, she worries him. He tries to stay within a certain radius of the apartment, which means that this freedom of his isn't freedom at all. He keeps returning just to check. One afternoon, he comes back from The Alibi to find her lying on the couch all curled up the way a match gets when you let it burn too long.

"I had a court date to get my baby back," she says. "And you weren't around to help me get there." She talks in a daze; the words dribble out. "I tried to call, but your phone's still off. You promised me."

Kid doesn't remember any court date, but he does know one thing and says it. "I didn't promise. Kid is not a promiser."

Then Pamela starts to squeak and cry. "I'm just here in the world and everyone else is so fucking, fucking, fucking fallen."

"Not me," says Kid. "I'm rising. I'm rising up!"

"You don't know what rising is or falling neither," Pamela says back. "Or what the TV is or what's really on it. You don't look for truth or what things mean even when you pretend to. It's all some trick. You make the quarter disappear even when it's still really there."

Kid decides not to listen to that. He pulls the gold bracelet from the pocket inside his white suit jacket and dangles it in front of her. "That's where I was just now," he says. "I was buying it for you." He makes his voice sound manly and hurt. "I was going to give it to you on Christmas Eve, but then I couldn't wait because I love you so much."

Pamela sniffs and wipes, applies her face stuff and makeup.

"I'll get your baby back, too," Kid says. "After Christmas or the New Year. After I get the job. They're keeping an eye on me. There will be people I can call."

Later, she's knocking on the bathroom door, wanting to know what he's doing in there. Kid stows the figure, opens the door.

She tells him he's smart, lucky, wonderful, and he knows from the way she says it that she wants to fuck around. But Kid is tired and craving and rigged on thoughts of his own bright future, a future in which his importance will finally be recognized, his indiscretions made sense of, a future against which Pamela's face looks a little too freckled, a little too dim.

KID IS OUTSIDE a golf shop on the corner of Lankershim and Blix thinking about the clubs inside that his father might love for Christmas. Christmas Eve is the day after tomorrow. Kid has just turned his cell phone back on. There are no messages from his father, though, and that is hard.

The two men working in the aqueduct have gone away. Kid is having doubts about whether his father is really involved with the DWP and whether the DWP is really doing what he thinks it is. Maybe the action figure is just an action figure, and the money was just chance, and the real reason his father and mother can't talk to him anymore is because he's stolen from them and lied to them and chopped up the Thanksgiving turkey yelling that it was their dead son.

Maybe no one is watching.

Kid wants to put more money in the action figure's hand,

test it again, but he's scared to. He hasn't slept in a long time. He sees a reflection of himself in the golf shop window that looks like a skinny ghost, but it isn't a clear reflection, just a window reflection, so its accuracy is hard to judge.

Then somebody is behind him talking. "You doing all right?" this somebody says. "You maybe don't seem so great."

"I do, though," says Kid. "I do seem great." He speaks automatically, before realizing that this somebody he's speaking to is Phil, who used to get loaded with him back in high school and whose parents are friends with Kid's.

"On my way to KFC," says Phil. "I was just walking by when I saw you. Want some chicken? On me."

"No," says Kid, "let's go somewhere nice. I'm buying. I've got money."

"How?" asks Phil. He's unsure, suspicious, full of small, sober concerns, so that Kid almost doesn't want to bother talking him into the whole thing, but for some reason does it anyway.

THEY GO TO Portnoy's, where Kid used to go back when he was dealing and rich. "Laurence!" he calls to one waiter, "Murizio!" to another. "How do you like the new suit?"

"Splendid!" they call back. "The new suit is splendid!"

—Which would be enough to set Kid right again if not for Phil with his grinny-sad face and AA ideas. Phil in a sport coat he had to borrow from the maître d' to get in here, so that he looks like one of those snorty bulldogs that people stuff into outfits. "Just working the steps," says Phil, "a day at a time." And things like that. Kid orders his favorite prime rib, but he's too disgusted with all this rehab stuff to eat. The whole soggy life of bottomless apology. "I'm sorry," you're made to say to your father and he's made to say he's sorry back, and there's no chance for greatness left. In recovery, you're a cripple. You're a contestant in the Special Olympics cheered for a ten-minute limp around the track.

"How are your parents?" Kid asks.

"It was my dad's birthday a couple days ago. Went down early and Mom made us breakfast. Waffles. I got him a fishing reel."

"That sounds really good." Kid makes a smile. Magnanimous, he thinks. Kid is magnanimous. "Your parents been in touch with my parents? Seen them at all?"

Phil stops, looks out the window over Kid's shoulder as if at a teleprompter set up on the sidewalk. "I don't think so," is what he finally says. "I don't know."

Kid waits a second before turning around, but if the teleprompter was there, it must have been wheeled away. It occurs to him that his meeting Phil today was no accident. It must have been fate or setup.

"I'm going over to my parents' place for Christmas Eve," Kid announces, decides.

Phil seems startled. Like maybe he's waiting for someone to roll the teleprompter back.

THEY GET OFF the bus at sunset. Kid carries a pile of colorful gifts, while Pamela skitters along next to him. There's a pair of diamond earrings for his mother, a fishing reel for his father. Gifts for his aunt and cousins too. He and Pamela spent the whole night wrapping in orange and red with green and purple ribbons bursting off, dripping down—five, six ribbons on every gift. He shaved using Pamela's makeup mirror, because he's stopped trusting that one in the bathroom. And now he imagines how he must look in that white suit with all those gifts: a Christmas vision who will give and give.

"Christmas," his mother would always say, "is when we put our unpleasantness behind us." And Kid is determined to do it, even with Pamela hyperventilating and sweating off that face she spent so much time putting on.

"The sky's so big here," she says, "like a whole new real estate."

"Look at yourself," Kid says. "Will you look at yourself?"

The house is ancient Greece or paradise, with columns and fountains and statues of perfect, naked human beings. It's a house announcing that you can make your life exactly how you want. It's the house that Kid grew up in. Very quiet, very clean. The walls bare of family photos and most of the interior decoration consisting of his mother's spare-time sculptures of giant, powerful hands, his father's hands, reaching up from end tables and bureaus, reaching up from out of the floor.

"What time were we invited for?" Pamela asks.

But what is the point of telling her that they weren't literally *invited*, that invitations can come through other, more metaphysical channels? "Pretty much now," is what Kid says as he steps up to the portico, which is really the same as a porch, though his father always used the more cultured-sounding word.

Behind him, Pamela puffs out a breath of relief to have a roof above her again. She's got her little mirror, is busy remaking her face. "No talking about your baby, okay?" Kid commands her. "Or about how nervous it makes you to be outside. Or anything about the Department of Water and Power." She's nodding, trying to be helpful. She's got the gold bracelet on. Loves it, she says.

Kid sets down the gifts, reaches into his coat pocket to touch the action figure he's decided to bring to keep himself calm and the money clip with four hundred dollars left. Then he reaches back to grip the handle of the Colt Super pistol he brought, too. Just in case. He takes a breath, rings the bell, feels the bigness of the moment—a father's son returned to him.

Kid listens for footsteps, but doesn't hear any.

He rings the bell again.

He raises a fist to hammer the door.

He looks into the window only to see a house emptied of everything. Even the curtains. There's only the reflection of the sunset, of himself, of Pamela back there doubting him.

He flips open his phone to call his father's number, but it's been disconnected. His mother's, too. He steps off the porch, leaving the gifts and Pamela there.

"Kid!" she yells. "Kid?" as if his name were a question.

He looks back at that small, panicked girl with her face falling in on her—falling in on him—and runs.

"EXCUSE ME. I just need to get that Barbie car."

"What?" asks Kid.

"The Barbie car. The roadster," says the man next to him at the Toys "R" Us. "It's for my daughter. Christmas. One last thing, and you're . . . standing right in front of it." The man wears a vest and tie. He's one of these multi-taskers, these nowaday power fathers.

"God," says Kid, "it's bright in here. Isn't it bright in here? Probably so the security cameras work better. But you feel like you're on an operating table. My dad's a surgeon. He does face transplants. Isn't that weird? Face transplants? It means you're one person but you're really someone else. My dad has tons of money, but he doesn't give any to me. No Barbie cars or other cars, either. Hey, let's go get a Christmas Eve drink." Kid flashes his money clip to prove how many Christmas Eve drinks he could buy if he wanted to.

But "Thank you, no," the father says. "I have to get home to my family." He's already reached past Kid for the Barbie car and now he's turning his back, striding his powerful stride away.

Kid's hand jumps for the pistol. He wants to blow this man's father-head into juice. But he's on camera; potential employers from the DWP could be watching even now. Self control, he thinks at them and reminds himself why he's here.

His father could never approve of someone like Pamela, young and helpless with a face she has to put on, a mockery of a transplant. Pamela the take-aparter, the disconnector, who trusts Kid so little she has to keep her car-wreck money in a safe, Pamela who ruined Thanksgiving and would have ruined Christmas, too, if Kid's father wasn't wise enough to keep it from happening, Pamela who isn't even a Pamela, but just a plain old Pam.

So Kid is here looking for a stronger, more independent girl. He'd like one with a nice round ass too, but the plastic windows of the Barbie boxes display only the fronts, and Kid must not linger in this pink aisle trying to peek around at the asses of dolls. He's pretending to be an uncle shopping for his niece, and he squints at the dolls the way he thinks an uncle might.

He's tempted by Veronica in a silver miniskirt and bouncy Shirley with her reassuring smile. Still, the bigness of these dolls in comparison to his action figure worries him, so he leaves this aisle and tries the other.

There aren't as many females in the action-figure aisle and they aren't as curvy, but Kid soon discovers Princess Natalie in a white gown with a knife in her belt and a hawk on her shoulder. So now he needs a car. That man, that father had given him the idea, had probably even been placed there to do it. The message is clear. Your father wants you to get a car, leave this place, find him.

But they don't have cars for action figures, only spaceships and dragons, things like that. And while Kid is looking for what might fit best, he sees the action figure of himself, packaged and with another name. Jim Healey in something called *Force Five*.

Kid reaches out, grabs it. "Jim Healey may look ordinary," he reads, "but don't let appearances fool you! He has super sight! Can withstand extreme environments! Breathe underwater and take dead aim with his pistol! Jim Healey's origin is as yet unknown. Is he the real son of Walter and Patricia Healey or the result of a top-secret government experiment?"

Kid looks up from the box, scans the other people in the aisle to see if any are watching, but none seem to be. Forgetting about Princess Natalie and the car, he looks through the other figures for maybe a Walter or Patricia Healey, but he just keeps finding more Jims. He finds a figure named Eclipse who's wearing something called the Belt of Orion. But there's only one Eclipse and twenty Jim Healeys, hanging there like babies in an adoption agency.

Kid takes down one at a time, studying each, loving each. He has no basket or shopping cart, so gathers them up in his arms.

NOW IT'S CHRISTMAS morning, and Kid sits on the floor of Bug and Lina's apartment, Jim Healeys scattered around him like opened-up presents.

He's studying the TV, but there isn't much on it. Just an empty courtyard. A swimming pool. Night.

Bug and Lina are hiding in the bedroom.

Kid came here directly from Toys "R" Us. It was late by then, and the front door stayed closed a long time after he knocked. But once it opened, there were all kinds of people inside, a Christmas party. "Come on in!" they told him, and with a giant relief, he did. He stowed his bag of Jim Healeys in the closet and spent the rest of his money buying all the meth, all the weed Bug had. "Kid's treat!" he announced. "Kid's Christmas gift!" He was the man in the white suit, the Christmas miracle. Lina and others told him that, and he told himself that, too. No need to worry, for I am the Christmas miracle.

Kid watched Bug's 3-D neon posters move and twist and make new meanings one after another, pulling the world together into something even more whole. The TV was on with the camera recording at however-many-hours' delay, so that as the party continued, people saw themselves arriving. "Come on in!" Kid would shout at those on-screen arrivals.

But later, when most of the people had already left, Kid came out of the bedroom to find the rest of them playing with his Jim Healeys. They had torn them from their boxes and were walking them across the carpet. "They're mine," Kid said. Or maybe he said, "They're me."

Lina, who was twisting the figures into a complicated,

self-fucking orgy, looked up at Kid, eyes gigantic from the meth he'd given her. "Dude," she said, "They *are* Kids. Check it out. They're little mini-Kids."

It got them all laughing. Kid blurted a quick story about how they were presents for his cousins and now they'd all been ruined.

"Relax," said Bug, which was what he always said when he'd done something wrong but wanted to make it sound like he hadn't. "Re-*laaaaax*," he said, pulling the word out long, which got Kid thinking about that front door closed so long against him. So Kid grabbed his Colt Super pistol and pointed it at Bug's head. Then everyone was serious.

It was a wonderful feeling. A wonderful, powerful feeling of everybody in his hands. And when Kid pulled the trigger there was no anger in it. Only glee.

But if Jim Healey was a dead aim with his pistol, Kid was not. The bullet missed Bug and exploded into one of the neon, meaning-shifting 3-D posters. People were yelling, scattering, but now Kid wanted to hit the poster, and he kept shooting, feeling better each time, and he couldn't believe how loud the gun was, how much it kicked in his hand, the gunshots pumping him up, spinning him out.

Soon the room was clear and Kid was out of bullets, the poster less torn up than he'd thought. Hoped.

He sat on the floor. Or maybe he fell on the floor. He is still here now. Here in front of the TV.

He flips open his cell phone and looks for messages. *Christmas*, he'd like to say to someone, to Pamela, *is when we put our unpleasantness behind us.* He remembers actually feeling that as a boy on Christmas morning, on the floor, presents scattered around him.

Then he remembers that he left Pamela stranded on that porch and knows he can't go back to her. He has no money or place to live, doesn't know what to do next. He tries a hit on the pipe, but like the gun, it's empty. The rest of the meth must be in the bedroom, or else someone has stolen it.

He picks one of the Jim Healeys off the floor, grabs his older, worn-down action figure and compares the two side by side. The results are inconclusive. He thinks about all the Jim Healeys in all the toy stores all over the country, the ones that have been bought and forgotten, the ones being played with now.

He looks at the TV again, hits fast-forward. The image is the same. He hits pause, hits play; it's all the same. An empty courtyard. A swimming pool. Night.

And then.

On the TV, a man appears. A man in a dirty white suit holding a Toys "R" Us bag. A thin-chested man with a bloated, starver's belly. A misaligned version of Santa Claus. He stands at the edge of the pool, looking down into it, maybe thinking about swimming or killing himself or trying to breathe underwater. Or else just looking for his reflection. He keeps rearranging his stance in quick, twitchy moves. After awhile, he looks up again and twitches his way toward the door, the peephole, the camera. He's an ugly man, a sick man, a dun-skinned corpse with poking eyes and a film of sweat thick as Saran Wrap.

He has Kid's face, but that doesn't mean he's Kid, since that face could be a transplant.

The man knocks. He waits. He knocks again. His hands hang small at the ends of his arms, and the knock he makes is quiet.

NO WOMEN TONIGHT

JIM AND I buzz along an edge of the Pacific Ocean in a dinghy, trying for the next harbor. Swell high. Moon gone.

Jim's up at the bow—thick, stubborn, drunk. Dangling his feet into the water and yelling how we're men. "White men in America! Lucky as fuck!"

Years ago, his older brother died in a car crash. Sometimes he uses that as a line with women. Sometimes it works.

Drinking can trigger his seizures, but he doesn't want to stop, and I tell myself that making people do things they don't want to isn't a part of my beliefs anymore.

"Keep hold of the rope," I say instead, and he asks me who I'd die for.

I give it some thought, tell him no one.

"No one? *No one?* Not your parents? Not your ex-wife? What kind of human being are you?"

"I don't know."

"I'd die for *my* ex-wife. I'd die for her. There's ten, fifteen people I'd die for at least. Maybe even you, you selfish shit."

"It doesn't count if you want to die anyway."

I think he'll be mad, but he laughs instead. "We're men, aren't we? Fucking men!"

"Yeah," I say, unable to match his enthusiasm. I'm closer to my own divorce than he is to his, and the guilt of my failure pulls hard.

A swell hits. Jim wobbles and tilts. He's twitching now and too far to reach. "Hold onto the rope!" He's not even a good swimmer.

We talked it all over before the trip, the way that grown men do. He said that if he had a seizure and fell into the Pacific, then I should go in after him, do my best. And no hard feelings either way.

ISLAND OF THE LOST BOYS

THE DISTANCE FROM Tempe, Arizona to Newport Beach, California is 379 miles. At sixty miles an hour along the 10 Freeway, it has taken Ted Asmund six hours and twenty minutes to get here. He has just crossed the bridge to the island and is parallel parking now. He checks his mirrors, cuts the wheel and inches back—all with a slow, deliberate precision that gives no hint at the state of his heart, which is beating so fast it might be the heart of some much smaller animal.

Ted Asmund wears a Hawaiian shirt tucked into a pair of pleated khakis and cinched with a shiny belt. He is thirty, with short legs and a long torso combining into a medium height. He isn't exactly ugly, but he gives off an awkward, unnatural quality that has prompted one of the students at Tempe Junior High School where Ted teaches math to call him *Mr. Asimo* or just *Asimo* after the robot built by Honda that can wave and get the newspaper. That student's name is Casey Miller, and yesterday at detention, for reasons he doesn't entirely understand, Ted tried to kiss him on the mouth.

All last night and all this morning, Ted kept reassuring himself that Casey wasn't the sort of boy to tell, and thus, the best thing would be to go into school and pretend nothing had happened. Ted got into his car at seven a.m. intending to do just that. But he found himself driving all the way out here to his mother's house instead. He thought he'd call the school along the way with a made-up story about being sick, but was never quite able to do it. Seventy-five miles in, he shut his cell phone off.

It is Thursday, November 10. The housecleaners work on Thursdays, and Ted's mother stays out doing errands until around two. But by the time Ted has himself suitably parked and out of the car, it's eighteen minutes after. He checks the garage for his mother's BMW and experiences some measure of relief to find it isn't there. He lets himself into the house. "Mom?" he calls out to the quiet, Pine-Soled air, "Mom?" just to be sure, before rushing upstairs to her bedroom.

The bedroom has just been remodeled for the third time since Ted moved out. The new carpet is beige shag. The bedside tables are shaped like hourglasses on which rest identical thin-screened clocks and identical vases each containing a single moist and suggestive orchid. The bed is canopied with red velvet curtains creating the effect of an altar or a stage. Variously sized mirrors crowd the walls, projecting images of the bed, orchids, vases, tables, carpet, and Ted Asmund himself infinitely in all directions.

Still, Ted doesn't much notice the remodel, because he is staring in panic at the blinking light on his mother's answering machine and thinking about the day he was hired, when he had written down her home phone number as an emergency contact. Eventually, he presses play, listens to a courtesy call from American Express, then to Max the jeweler reporting that the necklace Ted's mother had commissioned is finished and lovely. That is all.

Ted lets out a breath. He checks his watch. He steps downstairs to the living room and takes a seat on the couch. Back straight. Hands folded. Polite though he is alone.

The telephone doesn't ring. Does not and still does not.

At two fifty-three Ted hears the garage door groan. His mother is home.

ONE MIDNIGHT, BACK when Ted was Teddy and Teddy was six, his beautiful young mother awakened him to announce that they were saved. An entrepreneur named Raymond Misterly was going to marry her and be his father and take them away from their one-bedroom apartment in Tempe, Arizona to his two-story waterfront house on an island in Southern California.

Teddy didn't know what an entrepreneur was or much of what a father was, either. Still, he did know islands. Gilligan's Island. Tom Sawyer's Island. His mother started telling him something about her ring, but Teddy was already nearing sleep again, island-hopping his way there. Treasure Island. Fantasy Island. The Island of the Lost Boys.

Once a sandbar in a harbor, Newport Island was built up into a solid piece of land in the 1920's, then paved over and reinforced with seawalls. It is a small cluster of wealthy, suburban blocks surrounded by a channel—a beautiful place certainly, but quite developed, and whatever resemblance it came to have to those islands that so captured Teddy's imagination, whatever magic, had far less to do with the place itself than with the friend he met there.

Cannon appeared on the very first day the new family pulled up to the house. He was sitting on a red curb across the street without a shirt or shoes on, a boy all ready for summer.

"WHAT IS IT?" Ted's mother asks when she sees her son in the house. "Thanksgiving already? Cesar Chavez? Is that in the fall?   National-Show-Up-and-Surprise-Your-Mother-without-Calling-First-Day?" She smiles, flirtatious. "Hi, Teddy Bear."

They hug. Ted would like to pull her close, to fall on his knees and cry into her lap, but he is careful. Hugs her lightly and pulls away.

"I just needed some time off," he says, making a gesture toward the Hawaiian shirt. "You know how it can be." He had bought the shirt at a gas station on the way here in an attempt at making himself look like an easygoing vacationer.

But Ted's mother isn't paying his shirt any attention; she's looking at his face, her eyes skipping all over it while Ted tries to arrange a suitable expression. He read in a magazine once that a happy expression is the most difficult to fake, so he thinks happy thoughts—thoughts of his childhood with Cannon. And maybe it works, because soon his mother breaks off the examination.

"Oh, Teddy," she says, "of course I do. Now let me show you the remodel."

Ted checks his watch again, sees that it is two fifty-five, the time the kids go home and the administration starts on the unfinished business of the day: absence slips mostly, and telephone calls. "All right," he says. "I just need to get my luggage from the car," and he's out the door.

Of course, there is no luggage to get, because Ted hadn't planned to come here.

His car is a gray 2002 Toyota Echo—dependable, affordable, and fuel-efficient. Ted gets in and drives away.

RESTLESS AND PANICKED, he tells himself to go back to Arizona, to leave now before things get worse. Still, he can't find the resolve to do it. So he just keeps driving around. Past the public library and the place he used to rent videos that has since become a sandwich shop. Down to the beach, back to the island, off the island and up Cliff Drive to the house on the corner where

Cannon now lives with his family.

Cannon's two young daughters run around a playhouse in the yard, yanking and slamming the front door, sing-songing *mom-mee! dad-dee! bab-bee!* while the mother herself looks on holding her baby boy. The father, Cannon, whom Ted has not seen for well over a decade, must still be at work. It's a big house, but not gaudy. Ted has been at the stop sign for several minutes watching, and the mother has just now turned to notice.

Ted speeds away. He drives a few more blocks before pulling over across the street from Bay Shores Junior High where he himself used to go. He tries to catch his breath, regain his calm. The Bay Shores soccer team is just starting a scrimmage, shirts versus skins. The star of the skins' team is an energetic, ball-hogging left forward with short, dark hair and a way of moving through the game that announces his obvious superiority. It's a nice day out, the grass bright green, and the sky wide open. And watching that game, those boys, the grace of coordinated movement, the health and physics at work, the simple, enforceable set of rules, the agitated man does regain his calm. For a little while, at least.

LATER, TED IS eating dinner on the patio of his mother's house with she and Mr. Knowles. Whole grilled sea bass stuffed with shallots, garlic and basil. Mr. Knowles does all the cooking. He is a bigger, more jovial man than Ray Misterly, but similar in his way of loving Ted's mother: When she shifts her attention away from him and toward her son, her rosebushes, or the sunset on the water, Mr. Knowles simply sits and waits for its return.

"How's Arizona treating you, Ted?" he asks. Ted says that Arizona is treating him fine. And that is all from Mr. Knowles.

Ted's mother is talking about the remodel again. She loves this house, she says. It was the only thing she insisted on in the divorce. These days, she says, she doesn't feel any bitterness toward Ray at all, only gratitude to him for bringing them here, and what in the world her Teddy Bear is doing back in that grungy excuse for a city after she worked so hard to get them out of there is a thing she can't imagine.

Only fifteen when she had him, Ted's mother is in her mid-forties now and possibly more beautiful than ever, because in exchange for crow's-feet and a figure more earned than given, age has granted her an almost philosophical command of what that beauty is and can do. She is languid, feline, suggestive of length rather than height. Her A-line skirt was custom-made for her, but so too might have been the sunset reflecting from the water to set her off sparkling.

If it were possible to separate the face from its expressions, the body from its bearing, some real similarity might be found between this mother and the son who sits across from her. But then, it isn't. Their eyes may be the same shade of blue, but where there is ease and sensuality in hers, his are tight and nervous.

That long torso, so elegant on the mother, gives her son a look of teetering even while seated.

It is six thirty. No call has come for Ted and he should be safe until tomorrow, at least. He came through the door forty-five minutes ago ready with several excuses, but his mother didn't ask for them. She didn't address his disappearance at all, nor the fact of his not having the luggage he had said he was going to get two hours before. It was as if she didn't notice. *Flighty* is the word Ted uses to explain her behavior to himself. Flightiness, he believes, isn't *not* caring for others so much as the ability to care for others entirely on ones own terms—a basic entitlement of the beautiful. And though his mother's flightiness may sometimes be hurtful to Ted, it is nonetheless a quality he admires.

The sea bass is delicious, the sunset a good one, and Ted is trying hard to enjoy himself. His mother, once Ms. Asmund, once Mrs. Misterly, Ms. Asmund again briefly and now Mrs. Knowles, talks on about this or that, while husband and son attend—happy to be near her and grateful. They listen well. They lean in close. Because she is who she is and because she is beautiful and beauty is like that. Ted knows.

LATER THAT NIGHT Ted takes a walk around the island. It has changed from when he was Teddy, become even wealthier and more developed. And yet the island's present state has a certain translucence for him. Looking down at the smooth black asphalt that now paves the streets, he can almost see through it to the old cracked and dirty concrete. The Newport Island Park has been entirely re-landscaped, and there is no storage shed, but there used to be; a linden tree grew alongside it and spread its branches thickly over, so the boys could climb the tree to the roof of the shed to hide and whisper. They would sit close, bare feet dangling down, and sometimes Cannon would throw an arm around him. It was nothing out of the ordinary for boys to do—just touching before touching got complicated.

Some things are the same. Docks they used to fish from. The empty lot where Cannon had jumped down to the mud at low tide and Teddy had climbed after him.

Cannon was the leader and the reckless one and the one with ideas. He would steal Ho Hos and Snickers from the Vons just off the island, would cover golf balls in hairspray, light them on fire, and hit them over the channel into the neighborhood on the other side—all while Teddy stood by playing lookout and balancing fear with devotion.

If any other kid crossed the bridge, Cannon would lie to him that this was a private island and you needed a pass to be here. Then, if the kid didn't leave, even if it was someone they played with at school sometimes, Cannon would knock him to the ground. And though Teddy often felt sorry for the kid, there was an unspoken understanding between the two friends that this behavior was not unprovoked aggression so much as preemptive strike. A defense of what they had. Their island.

Ted Asmund circles that island, or what that island has become, seven times before returning to his mother's house. Her bedroom door is open, and inside he can see her and Mr. Knowles asleep in the canopy bed, tangled in some complicated but comfortable-looking embrace.

In his own bedroom—the only part of the house that has never been remodeled—Ted removes his shoes and socks. Unbuttons his Hawaiian shirt and finds a hanger for it. Places his wallet, keys and watch on the bedside table.

He finds a spare toothbrush in the bathroom and brushes his teeth without looking into the mirror, as if it were someone there he has never met before and feels shy of.

He lies down in his twin bed, turns off the light and tries to sleep while his mind strays into territories he wishes it wouldn't.

THE SUMMER BEFORE Cannon and Teddy started at Bay Shores Junior High, an old man on the island died and his house was left vacant. So the two boys recovered a beanbag couch from an alley dumpster. Cannon brought over his stereo, Teddy his TV and VCR, and the two boys created a hideout far more glorious than the roof of the storage shed at the park.

Eventually, Cannon started to coordinate small parties at the dead man's house with beer he stole out of people's garages.

Girls arrived peddling Schwinn cruisers with bare feet. And there was a boy named Rob, who Cannon used to throw rocks at, but suddenly seemed to like.

Cannon's wanting this hideout to be different from those that came before it—shared with the other kids instead of defended from them—wasn't a problem for Teddy. Though some part of him wished that things could stay exactly as they were, he had nonetheless been made to understand through filmstrips and playground talk that it was normal for pubescent boys and girls to interact. So by the beginning of summer when they were putting the hideout together, Teddy began to look forward to the twists and turns, the drama and romance that such interaction would offer.

Still, when the time came, Teddy couldn't seem to figure out how this interaction was performed. Here was Cannon. Here was Rob. Making small talk, telling jokes. And then here was Teddy. Sitting on the beanbag couch in his Quicksilver shorts and new Nike shoes feeling his head go empty and his face go red. Here was Teddy taking tiny sips off a single beer to keep himself from getting drunk and losing control. Here he was trying to make up for having nothing to say by nodding and laughing along with whatever conversation was already going on.

One night Cannon and Rob were joking about how everything was in their pants. When the girl they'd brought over said she wanted another beer, Cannon said the beer was in his pants. And when the girl said they should put on something else to listen to, Rob said there was something else in his pants.

"Me too," said Teddy.

"Huh?" asked the girl.

"There's something else in my pants too. You should see, um, what it is."

It was the same thing Cannon and Rob had just been saying, but the reaction was entirely different. "John, man," said the girl—John was Cannon's first name, and he had just started to use it—"John, man, your friend's getting all creepy on me."

Often Cannon would make out with one of the girls who came over. Their hands explored and held each other's bodies. Teddy would look and then look away.

It seemed to the boy that since his mother was poised and beautiful, these qualities must eventually surface in him too. But then there was his biological father, about whom he knew nothing. Teddy waited for his mother to tell him about his father, waited to find the courage to ask.

His mother wasn't home much those days. She had just started working at Knowles' Real Estate. ("I need something to do," she had explained to Teddy and Ray Misterly at dinner, "something for me.")

Teddy bought a book called *The Ultimate Secrets of Total Self-Confidence* and kept it under his mattress the way other boys did pornography.

He saw Cannon less frequently over the next year and

thought about him more. How handsome he had suddenly become. How popular. And sitting near him during lunchtime at school or knocking on his door—"Hello, Mrs. Cannon, is Cannon around?"—behaviors that used to be so natural for Teddy had suddenly become things he had to talk himself into or out of.

TED ASMUND LIVED at his mother's house all the way through the University of Irvine, where he earned a degree in math and a teaching certificate. When he finally did leave home, it was less because he wanted to than because he knew it was the adult thing to do, and over time he has managed to taper his visits down to three or four per year.

Ted Asmund has chosen a career that matches his interest in math with the satisfaction of doing good in the world. He earns a small but dependable income and is thrifty with money. He has found a doctor, a dentist, a mechanic, and an accountant he can trust. He listens to Dr. Laura Schlessinger on the radio and tries to apply the advice she gives to his own life. He keeps a day planner to schedule activities ranging from cleaning the toilet to grading exams to researching the ethics of large corporations so that he may avoid certain products that exploit the peoples of third world countries. There is a word of the week in his day planner and he tries to use this word at least three times during that week so he will remember it. On Tuesdays, Thursdays and

Saturdays, he jogs four miles and has recently taken up yoga after overhearing a very convincing conversation in the teachers' lounge.

Ted Asmund may not be the absolute best teacher at Tempe Junior High, but he is certainly the most patient, willing to explain a concept repeatedly until it is understood and ready to listen should a student need a sympathetic ear. He has always believed in treating his students with the respect given to peers, and as a point of principle, he does not to refer to them in any demeaning terms, not even in his head.

Ted Asmund looks a person in the eye upon shaking his or her hand. He is friendly to co-workers, making an effort to ask about topics that he knows interest them, from informing Mrs. Walstien about a sale at Bed, Bath and Beyond to commenting on a Suns game to Mr. Phelps and saying that Steve Nash is "a very *dexterous* player."

Ted Asmund lost his virginity three years ago to a woman named Linda whom he met on the Internet. She was several years older than he and talked a great deal about how a woman in her forties was at her sexual peak—even during the act itself. The act wasn't quite what Ted had hoped it might be. And when Linda climbed out of bed in the middle of the night and started getting dressed, he pretended to be asleep because he wasn't sure how to behave. He didn't much mind her going, but it had somehow been his understanding that a woman disappearing like that would leave something behind to remember her by—her underwear, a friendly note—and he was disappointed to find that she hadn't.

Nothing had ever happened with Cannon. Nothing in particular. The boys just grew apart. Or Cannon just grew apart from him. The friendship ended seventeen years ago, and Ted Asmund has not found another one since.

ON WEDNESDAY, OCTOBER 6, Casey Miller suggested to Mr. Asmund that since there was no one else at detention, the two of them should play a few games of World Cup Soccer on the Nintendo Game Boy. "I brought this cord," he said. "You can hook two of them together."

Ted had confiscated a total of six Game Boys from Casey along with several cartridges, MP3 players, issues of *Sports Illustrated* and *Rolling Stone*, and a plastic grabber with a Tyrannosaurus Rex head on the end that the boy had been clamping onto Laura Delmino's breasts. He was a difficult student from a wealthy family, a student who amazed and confounded Ted with how little he seemed to care—about the class and his performance in it, about his teacher as a figure of authority, about other people in general. On his exams, Casey would do the first problem, maybe the second and then write, "DON'T KNOW ASIMO!" in robot letters across the rest.

"C'mon," Casey said. "I know you're a soccer fan. I've seen you watching me play. I'm good, huh?"

Ted was not really much of a soccer fan—not at that

point, anyway—but the field was on the way to the faculty parking lot, and after school on his way home, Ted had paused to watch at least often enough to know that Casey's claim to be good was an understatement; he played sweeper and was easily, effortlessly the best on the team.

"I won't tell," said Casey, "I promise." He had on a white t-shirt, and his dark blond hair was cut or uncut in such a way as to fall down over his eyes.

Against his better judgment, but thinking through the school guidelines and finding nothing that expressly forbade a teacher from playing video games with a student after regular school hours, Ted walked over to the propped open door of his classroom, looked left down the hall, right, left again, and closed the door.

Casey beat him twenty-six to nothing that first game, talking the whole way through. "Think you're so hot at math, Asimo, *ha*, look at *this*," he would say, all his boy's grace transferred into that pixilated team. A steal, a pass, a bicycle kick to score, while Ted's goalkeeper just twitched and wandered in circles.

ON SATURDAY, NOVEMBER 12 at eight-thirty in the morning, Ted sits in the bleachers at Bay Shores Junior High watching a peewee game. It is cool, but sunny enough to have dried the dew from the grass.

Yesterday Ted's mother had finally noticed that he

didn't have any luggage, and instead of asking why, she took him shopping. While his mother was in the Neiman Marcus dressing room, a young female employee complimented Ted on his stunning, sophisticated wife. This tends to happen when they are together, and neither Ted nor his mother ever correct the mistake, but take the compliment as it is given.

Now in a new gray shirt with French cuffs and brown slacks nano-technologically altered neither to wrinkle nor to stain, now cheering along with the parents in the bleachers, Ted is enjoying the thought that he might be mistaken for a parent himself, a businessman who goes into the office on Saturdays, but finds a way to make it to his daughter's games. Someone like Cannon has become.

The peewee game ends one-zero on a goal made by a boy against his own team. No one seems to mind, though, least of all the boy himself, who is holding an orange slice in his mouth and imitating a monkey while his father runs a careless hand into his mess of hair. Down from the bleachers and with no child to congratulate, Ted feels conspicuous. He pretends to talk on his cell phone, which is still turned off.

On the way home from the shopping trip yesterday, thinking about the message that might be waiting on the answering machine, angry and confused at his own continuing inability to call the school with some explanation for his absence, Ted opened his mouth to speak. Eventually what came out was a request for his mother to please call him Ted instead of Teddy. It was not what he had wanted to say. Or else it was only a very small part.

The single message on the machine that afternoon was from Ray Misterly, who lives alone nearby and still calls for Ted's mother sometimes.

Now, beyond the bright crowd of families and jerseys and coolers of oranges and Gatorade, out in the empty North field, two boys from the Bay Shores team arrive. Ted had not known whether they would be playing at home today, and he finds himself jittery with excitement. Still, he doesn't go over immediately, but allows time for some other boys to arrive and some parents too. He sees the star from Thursday's scrimmage moving along the sidewalk toward the North gate.

A ball is produced, a circle formed. The boys juggle the ball; they pass it and laugh and go for dramatic diving saves that send them to the ground.

ACCORDING TO HIS day planner, Ted Asmund was supposed to have spent October 6 correcting Exam #3 for his Algebra classes, picking up a new ink cartridge and a packet of 3x5 cards, and speaking to his landlord about the drainage problem in the shower. Instead he brought one of Casey Miller's confiscated Game Boys home, found some tips on the Internet and stayed up until two-thirty in the morning practicing. The scores that next day at detention were fifteen to one Casey, twelve to nothing Casey, and ten to three Casey.

"Hey, Asimo."

"Hello, Casey, how are you today?"

"Ready to kick your ass at World Cup Soccer's how I am."

It was like that. Ordinary, familiar, and probably the best month in all of Ted Asmund's adult life.

Sometimes Casey told him things that might be seen as inappropriate for a student to tell a teacher. How he had sold some chopped up parsley to a kid in his third period telling him it was marijuana. How Katy Brewer and Mark Salisman had had sex when her parents were away and, not having a condom, used a Ziploc bag. Or how Mr. Anders put all the good-looking girls in the front row, and the ones who wore short skirts always got A's.

"Y'know," said Casey, "participation grade." He could be clever, sarcastic. Ted had the feeling the boy's parents ignored him.

They couldn't play World Cup Soccer every day, since Casey didn't always have detention and sometimes other students were there. But gradually, the other students seemed to earn detention less while Casey seemed to be going out of his way for it. He blatantly cheated on quizzes and was even more smart-alecky in class, an entirely different person from the one who

Ted saw later in the day. The complexity of this behavior, of Casey's mocking him on the one hand while earning detention to be with him on the other, was something Ted thought about probably more than he should have. There were other thoughts, too. That Casey's hair was the color of nothing else in the world, for example, or that he had not one way of flipping it away from his eyes, but several, each communicating a slightly different mood.

Algebra Exam #3 went uncorrected and the shower drain only got worse. The placeholder in Ted's day planner didn't move past the week of October 4-10. The word of that week was *vertiginous.*

After detention, Ted would try to look as stern and teacherly as possible as he walked Casey out to a soccer practice already half over. Ted usually went straight home after that, but a few times—and the sheer imprudence of this behavior is stunning to him now—he had taken a seat in the bleachers pretending to correct quizzes while he watched. There were usually some girlfriends in the bleachers too, and girls who wanted to be girlfriends, and some kid or other still waiting for his mother to pick him up.

THE BAY SHORES game is scoreless until half time. But the opposing team scores almost immediately after kickoff in the second half and then again on a penalty kick for a foul committed by the star.

Bay Shores gets sloppy then and can't seem to get the ball out of their side of the field. They lose two to one. After the game there is a conflict between the coach and the star, who storms off through the North gate cussing all the way.

Ted's Echo is parked near the South gate. He puts his hands in his pockets and whistles his way back toward it.

He drives slowly along Clay Avenue, stopping at each intersection to peer down side streets. The star must live close by if he walked to the game, Ted is thinking, and he might already be home by now drinking a Coke or taking a shower or drinking a Coke in the shower. When Ted gets to Fullerton Street without seeing the star, he takes a left and then loops back up Beacon Avenue.

And there he is, in Ted's rearview mirror, walking the opposite way. Ted executes a three-point turn and drives up behind the star. He slows, rolls down his window and lets out a cheery hello. "Listen, what happened over there? Is there anything I can do?"

The star turns his head. This is the first time Ted has seen his face up close. It is sharp and pimply, a face used to sour expressions like the one it wears now as it registers the fact that this man in the Echo is no one he knows.

"I'm . . ." Ted continues, thrown off, "My daughter plays on the peewee team. Little Wendy. But then, you know, I needed some real soccer. I'm a lover of the game. A recent lover. I don't know a whole lot about it, but you know I'm . . . I'm *fervent.*"

Up until this point, Ted has been telling himself that his intentions toward the star are entirely pure, that because he is a teacher and has some practice listening to adolescents' problems, he might listen to this boy's too. But something about that sour face tells Ted otherwise. Something ugly and accusatory. Something afraid that makes Ted afraid too. And nervous. And angry. And full of a desperate, winded feeling of missing Casey Miller.

The star breaks into a sprint.

Ted accelerates after him. The star turns into an alley too narrow for the car. Ted pulls his Echo to the curb, unbuckles his seatbelt, rolls up his window, unlocks his car, gets out, and locks it again. And by the time Ted makes it to the alley, the star is gone.

THAT ONE GOOD month with Casey Miller had ended three days ago after their World Cup Soccer game went into a shoot out that tied and then on to another that Casey won by a shot Ted's goalkeeper dove for and missed. There was a high-five, a pause.

And then Ted closed his eyes, leaned in and hoped for the best.

He felt himself yanked and rearranged, the joints in his arms and shoulders turned in hard, unfamiliar ways, and only somewhere in the middle of all this did his lips brush against some part of Casey's warm young skin. Maybe his neck or the inner part of a forearm.

Then Casey had him in a headlock. "Whoa, Asimo," he said. "Relax."

Ted tried to relax while Casey squeezed his head. "I'm sorry," Ted managed to say. "I'll give you an A . . . in my class. It's . . . the least I can do." He added something about how teaching was his life.

Casey didn't say anything, just let go of Ted, who fell on the ground. He went to Ted's desk, stuffed his backpack with all the confiscated Game Boys, cartridges, MP3 players, the magazines and grabber. Then he left. The door clanked shut behind him.

Ted doesn't remember how long he lay on the floor. There is a gap in his memory from the point when Casey left the room to the point when he, Ted, found himself at his desk grading Algebra Exam #3. He stayed in his classroom catching up until 9:30 that night, long after soccer practice had ended.

It was not so much the idea of getting caught that made Ted unable to come into school the next day. It was the idea of Casey himself. Ted could imagine him hiding the word "faggot" inside coughing fits all through fifth period and tossing his hair from his eyes in that side-winding, superior way he did after a good play in either Game Boy Soccer or else the real thing.

"HELLO, MRS. CANNON. Is Cannon around?"

It isn't what Ted meant to say, and the Mrs. Cannon he's just said it to is someone else now—not Cannon's mother, but his wife. Back when she went to high school with them, her name was Amy Wilgoroth, and boys used to write that name on their desks next to lewd and romantic things. Now the new Mrs. Cannon stands in the doorway of that house on the peninsula holding her sleeping baby boy and regarding Ted perplexedly.

"Are you looking for John?" she asks.

Ted has come directly from the side of the road at Beacon Avenue where he had some kind of breakdown after the star ran off. There was crying, self-pity, hyperventilation, and Ted is certain that evidence of all this shows. Still, he stands up straight, reminds himself of his French cuffs and nano-technological slacks, and says, "Yes. I'm. Teddy, Ted, Ted Asmund. I used to be your husband's best friend when we were young."

He gives her time to recognize his name. He hasn't seen her since high school and hardly knew her then. Cannon didn't know her much then either, as far as Ted understands it, and so wouldn't have even had an opportunity to point out his old friend. Still, Ted has imagined that Cannon must have told her something about him since. In fact, he has imagined it in some detail. Husband and wife in bed together on a Sunday morning, and Cannon talking about jumping down to the mud or hitting those flaming golf balls across the channel.

But nothing like that seems to have happened, or if it did, it had been entirely forgettable. Ted can tell his name doesn't sound familiar to the new Mrs. Cannon by the effort she puts into making it seem otherwise. "Oh, Ted!" she says. "Of course! I'm sure he'd love to see you, Ted, but he's at the electronics store right now."

Ted appreciates that effort of hers. He really does. A lot of those pretty girls in high school weren't nice to guys like him, but she always was.

The younger of the two girls Ted had seen in the yard shuffles into the doorway wearing flip-flops and a Snow White dress.

"This must be Wendy," Ted says. "Hello there, Wendy."

The girl ignores him, bumps her forehead against her mother's hip. The baby boy wakes up. He yawns in that innocent way they have.

"Can I take a message, Ted?" Mrs. Cannon asks. "Do you want to leave a phone number? I don't have a pen on me right now, but if you'll just . . ."

"No. Thank you," Ted interrupts.

"Are you sure?"

"Yes. Thank you. You have very cute children. Maybe you can just tell him I said that, okay? Tell him Teddy says he has very cute children."

The house is spacious inside and comfortable-looking.

Earth tones, wide-open rooms and good natural light. Mrs. Cannon thanks Ted for the compliment, tells him she will pass it on and that it was nice to meet him.

In the driveway is a giant white S.U.V. with five decals on the back window, cartoon-like renditions of the family members. Beneath each figure of a child is a name—Gwen, Wendy and Tyler—but the parents are called Mom and Dad. Dad is wearing a shirt and tie; his sleeves are rolled up. He is smiling; they are all smiling. His arms are not entirely at his sides, but hang out a bit as if to say, "Here I am. This is me," or to offer a fatherly hug. Also in the tinted window is a reflection of Ted, blurred and behind them in the dark.

NOW IT IS Sunday morning at eleven-fifteen. Ted has told his mother and Mr. Knowles that he will be packing up his new clothes and leaving for Arizona today, but he has been trying to find the will to get out of bed for the past three hours. He has gone through several arguments to try to do so and is just getting back to how a journey of a thousand miles starts with a single step when the telephone rings.

Ted doesn't think much of it at first, since he's been assuming that the call could only come during school hours. But in the long pause after he hears his mother say hello, a tightness in his stomach informs him that this assumption has been naïve— that for something so important, something that might involve the police, a call could come anytime.

"Just a second," he hears her say, and soon she is knocking on his door. He climbs out of bed. His mother is holding her hand over the receiver and there are questions in her face.

He wants to answer those questions, but doesn't know what the answer would be. He might say that he wasn't aware of being attracted to adolescent boys when he took the job at Tempe Junior High and that he isn't sure when and how all the ways Casey Miller flipped his hair out of his eyes changed from an observation to a thing he thought about at night. He might tell her about his childhood with Cannon and about their growing apart. What it was like to lose his virginity to a woman ten years older who didn't leave a note behind, or what it was like to eat his tuna sandwich at an empty table in the teachers' lounge. He might ask her who his father was.

He imagines a long, mature conversation. Not here in his underwear with the phone between them, but dressed in some of those nice clothes she bought him, alone with her out on the patio during a magnificent sunset. He imagines her understanding him in a way that he is unable to understand himself.

But they aren't out on the patio, and there isn't time for all that now. Ted takes the phone and covers the receiver with his hand as she'd just been doing with hers. He feels the need to apologize. Not only for what he has done, but even more for not turning out the way she, or any mother, would have wanted.

What he finally does say to her, after a few false starts and with a feeling close to relief, is that he is in love.

Then he puts the telephone to his ear. "Hello? This is Ted Asmund speaking."

THAT SUMMER ON Newport Island between elementary school and junior high started out so well. Cannon and Teddy had found the old man's vacant house, and there were a few weeks in July before any other kids were invited over, when the two were still making plans and nothing had yet changed between them. "No one at Bay Shores has a place like we got—their own place to party," Cannon would say, "probably not even the eighth graders, so they'll want to be friends with us too."

We, said Cannon. *Us.*

The night before their first party at the house, the two of them discovered a box of unlabeled videotapes in the dead man's attic, so they tried out each in the VCR to see if any were pornography. None were, but there was an R-rated movie about a French butcher. Every time a beautiful woman came into his shop, the butcher would pretend he couldn't see which cut of meat she was pointing to, forcing her to lean down so that he could get a look at her breasts.

"Oh, yes," the butcher would say in subtitles. "Very choice selections. Very fine specimens."

It was funny. Really funny. Maybe about the funniest

thing they had ever seen.

Overlaying the movie, in the glass of the TV set, Teddy could see a reflection of his friend and himself together on the beanbag couch. The convex surface warped the image and made it look far off, so that judging from the reflection alone they might not have even been kids anymore, but grown-ups.

It might have been twenty years in the future. The house might have been one of theirs. And maybe Teddy had become an inventor and Cannon a professional stuntman. It was a vision of potential sweeping from this moment to tomorrow night's party and onward, as if what their parents and teachers were always telling them had to be true: that these two boys, these two friends, laughing together on the beanbag couch, they could grow up to be anyone. Anything.

TRANQUILITY

ON THE SEVENTY-FIFTH day of their marriage, halfway through his six o'clock vodka tonic, Clare Barlow's husband Rod announced that he had invited a woman over for dinner.

"A client?" Clare asked.

"No. The new front desk girl for my physical therapist."

A pause. Clare thought. And then she said, "I don't think there's enough ahi salad for three."

"You never finish your dinner anyway."

"I had a light lunch."

"No problem," said Rod. "I'll share mine." He finished off his drink, put the glass down on the kitchen table in that decisive way of his that made him an effective copy machine salesman, and went into the bedroom to change.

They had married on April 17th and moved south from Kingsland, Georgia fifty-eight miles to Tranquility, Florida, an entire community built by the Reprodux Companies for its employees and anyone wanting "a unique combination of traditional American charm and modern American ingenuity." The Barlows' one-story, two bedroom home was so sensibly laid out that it took no time at all to settle into. The leather sofa and easy chair, the golden oak dresser, the Van Gogh print, the large and small electric choppers, the antique pendulum school clock—each fell into place as simply and satisfyingly as a telephone into its cradle.

So by early June when the decorating was finished, Clare found herself with very little to do. Not that she minded. As a matter of fact, it was nice just to sit outside in their small wrought iron gazebo drinking iced tea and looking out over the construction of Colonial-style mansion units on the other side of New Walden Pond. She exchanged friendly waves with the workers. She read baby magazines with articles like "The Ten Great Fetus Foods" or "The Truth About the Baldness Gene." She congratulated herself on having brought down her Sobritol dosage to one fifty-milligram capsule before bedtime and thought of how proud her psychiatrist Dr. Judy Wimsatt must be. She counted the days she had been married: fifty-five, fifty-six, fifty-seven.

When Rod came home and asked what she had done all day, she would joke, "You know—Babies 101!" When he reminded her that it was important to enjoy being married awhile before starting a family, she would say, "And I'm enjoying it very much, thank you, Rod," then give him a kiss on the cheek. Sixty, sixty-one, sixty-two. Once in awhile, she would try to convince

Rod to eat dinner out in the gazebo, and he would refuse on the grounds that it made him feel like he was in jail. Sometimes she would give him a marriage count. Seventy-two, seventy-three, seventy-four.

And then, suddenly, this.

Clare opened the door to a small young thing in high heels. "Um, sorry?" the young thing said. "I'm looking for Rod Barlow? Bald guy?"

Clare introduced herself as Rod's wife and offered a handshake, but the young thing stepped back, wobbling on her heels. "Is this some kind of swingy thing?" she asked. "I mean, I don't want to put down anybody's chosen lifestyles or anything like that, but I guess I just sort of believe in true love. Y'know?"

Clare wanted to say that she did too—that as a matter of fact she and Rod were *in* true love and that she herself really didn't understand what this whole thing was about, either. But then it was also important to say all that in just the right way. Casually. And Clare wasn't so sure she *could* say it casually.

As it turned out, though, she didn't get the chance to try, because Rod rushed out from behind her and delivered up to that young thing one of those famously warm hugs of his. "Mickey, Mickey! Welcome, welcome!" he shouted. So that whatever awkwardness the young thing was feeling, whatever doubt, seemed to suddenly vanish.

The way Rod could put a person at ease was really

something to see.

"JEEZ," SAID MICKEY at dinner when she noticed all the *Be My Baby, American Baby* and *Sweet Nine* magazines stacked there on the hutch, "how many months are you?"

"I'm not pregnant yet," Clare told her. "It's important to enjoy being married awhile before starting a family." And she might have added her little joke about Babies 101 if Rod hadn't just then wrinkled his chin at her. It was an ugly expression, and it always made Clare's stomach drop. Still, she was hoping that with some effort over the years it might develop into one of those little quirks that old happy couples love about each other.

Now Mickey was telling her the story of how she and Rod had met just a few hours ago. "He was our last client today? See we left at the same time and we were driving next to each other on Less Traveled Road? And like I pass then he passes then we're stopped at a light and I look over? And he's made this note that he's holding against the window? And we're both in our cars, right? But it says, 'Need a ride?'"

"Rod's a real people person," Clare said. She expected Mickey to do the polite thing then and ask how she herself had first met Rod. But the young thing didn't. She went on to other topics instead, and Rod went right along with her. Clare would have very much liked to pay attention to what those other topics were, but couldn't because she was too busy trying to finish her huge portion of ahi salad. And Rod's having made her stomach drop by wrinkling his chin at her a few minutes ago wasn't helping. Clare ate in small bites. She took deep breaths and tried to think of pleasant things. Of the tree house they would order from the Tranquility Catalogue on their baby's eighth birthday. Of the calm on the surface of New Walden Pond.

Clare finished the ahi salad, but hours later, after the young thing had left, her stomach still hurt, and she thought it would be a good idea to add an extra fifty-milligram capsule of Sobritol to the one she took before bed along with her birth control pill and a hundred milligrams each of calcium, folic acid and Vitamin C. "A hundred of everything and zero babies," she said to Rod, who was on the bedroom floor stretching his back. But he didn't seem to hear her. Not that Clare minded for her own sake, but she did think he might like to know about the addition, since that much Sobritol would no doubt put her to sleep soon, so if he wanted to make love to her he'd better get to it.

She climbed onto the bed and leaned over to fuss with the pillows, causing her nightgown to inch up her thighs. Clare knew she was beautiful and saw no reason to pretend differently. Fair skin, sharp eyebrows, blond hair that did well in all humidities, a femininely muscular back. Her only real weak point was her feet, which were so flat they looked like a seven-year-old's drawing of feet. But everyone has crosses to bear, she reflected, and if ugly feet was one of hers, well, she was woman enough for the burden.

Clare had made up little pet names for each of Rod's back stretches. He was on Superman, for instance, when she stopped fussing with the pillows and slid under the sheets with the little sailboats on them. She waited through Upsy-Downsy, Yo-yo, Elephant, and by Bendy Straw, the Sobritol had begun to take effect.

She felt like a gate that had come unlatched in a breeze or a house with an open window.

She imagined herself answering the question that young thing Mickey hadn't bothered to ask: What's that? Oh, in a supermarket. That's right, I was looking for a fresh cantaloupe. You can never tell with cantaloupe. Anyway, up came Rod. "I'm a man," he said, "but if I had to, y'know, switch, then I'd want to look just like you." It was the most romantic thing I'd ever heard. And so confident you'd think he wasn't bald at all. Yes, a lucky woman. I know it. I even remember what he had in his shopping basket that day—a *Sports Illustrated* Swimsuit Issue, two apples, a twelve-pack of hot dogs and an eight-pack of buns, poor thing.

"Rod?" said Clare.

"Yeah," said Rod from the floor.

"Did you notice how everything that girl said sounded like a question? I don't imagine someone like that can have a whole lot of self-confidence."

"If you don't like her we don't have to invite her back. I just thought you might want a friend. Something to take up your time instead of baby magazines."

"It's not that I don't like her, Rod. I like her just fine. I was only making an observation is all."

Clare felt too tired to lift her head, but she managed to scoot back against the pillow and headboard, propping herself up just enough to see Rod performing the Human U—feet in the air and hands straining to meet them. It was the last stretch in his routine. Clare was really struggling against sleep by now and talking seemed the best way to do it, but she didn't want to talk about that girl anymore, so she just said, "The Human U." It didn't mean anything, but that night it might have been some kind of incantation, a one-time, personal abracadabra. Because no sooner had she said it than her husband snapped off the light and started making love to her.

AND THAT, CLARE thought, was that.

But a week later came Beth from the post office. Then Cynthia from four doors down. And Susan who could have been a model, but chose international banking instead.

"Do you like her?" Rod asked after each had left.

"She's certainly very beautiful."

"But do you like her?"

"You know who I like, Rod, is you."

"Well, *I* think she's nice."

"Me too, Rod. You know I do. Maybe I'm just too happy with my little life to start needing friends. It's like that movie *The*

Blue Lagoon. Fifty-eight miles from anyone we know. Really the only thing I mind about it is being so far away from Dr. Wimsatt. I really don't need anything else at all. Just you, me and our nice little home."

Yvonne winked at her every time Rod made a joke. Vera ate the baby carrots in a very suggestive manner. "Rod is the most principled person I know," Clare told her. "Commitment is very important to him. He waited until he was thirty-seven to get married because he had to make sure he was ready for 'the final commitment.' That's what he calls it: 'the final commitment.'"

Clare would sit in the easy chair, while Rod and the woman in question sat together on the sofa. He would have his six o'clock vodka tonic, and the woman in question would usually have a gin and tonic. He would start with a light news item or a dirty joke, and by the time they arrived at the dining room table, Rod and the woman were well into a bottle of Merlot and so involved in confessing the worst thing they'd ever done to a friend or debating the physical superiority of the black athlete that neither had a word to spare for Clare or the dinner she'd made them.

Clare didn't drink and people made her nervous. So every time Rod invited a woman to dinner she took an extra fifty milligrams of Sobritol. She started keeping it in the liquor cabinet next to Rod's vodka as a sort of joke. Ten minutes before the woman in question was expected to arrive, Clare would say,

"Well, time to hit the bottle."

Joan was a graduate student in something called Pop Studies. Her thesis had to do with subliminal sexual messages in Disney movies. "Come on," she said to Clare, "The Witch's nose? Sleeping Beauty's tower? *Seven Dwarves?* Come *on.*"

The baby magazines stopped holding Clare's attention, and instead she drew portraits of what their baby might look like. She drew babies with Rod's royal nose and babies with his left dimple. She drew babies with her own sharp eyebrows and small mouth. She drew composite features, mixing, say the height of her forehead with the roundness of his. She drew boys. She drew girls. Under each portrait she wrote notes: "Strong chin=inner strength (me)" or "Deep set eyes=unpredictable side (Rod+me)." Clare had always been artistic, so the portraits were easy for her, relaxing. And it was astounding to see all the possible variations created by mixing Rod's attributes and hers. All those necks. All those noses.

She drew several portraits a day and kept them in a manila folder behind the ironing board in the hall closet.

Miss Kim appeared unexpectedly before Rod had come home from work and hopped up on the counter while Clare was chopping shallots. Reaching for the coriander, Clare noticed that Miss Kim wasn't wearing any panties and that her private region was completely shaven. So instead of asking Miss Kim what country she was from, Clare decided to wash down one hundred and fifty milligrams of Sobritol with as much vodka as she could swallow.

THEN IT WAS 10:46 in the morning. Clare was sweating under the sheets with the sailboats on them and the telephone was ringing. It was Rod. He skipped right over the usual hi-how-are-you and hit the ground running with a long, eloquent lecture about how dangerous it was to mix Sobritol with alchohol, and how he had been calling since eight this morning, and did she know that she had been asleep for sixteen hours, which was practically comatose? If she hadn't picked up that time, he said, he would have called an ambulance.

Clare had to work so hard just to keep up with the conversation that she didn't have any control over where it went. Rod said he probably would have strained his back carrying her to bed if Judy—that was Miss Kim's first name—if Judy hadn't been kind enough to help. He told her to take two birth control pills this morning since she hadn't been able to take one last night, and that they had better not make love for a week to be on the safe side. He said he had a client on the other line so they would have to talk when he got home.

After three ibuprofen, a shower, a muffin and a glass of orange juice, Clare went out to the gazebo to draw baby portraits. When the heads all came out lopsided, though, she found herself fending off a potential panic attack about birth defects with a capsule of Sobritol, which led in turn to another potential attack when she realized there were only twelve capsules left in the bottle. She called to schedule an appointment with Dr. Judy Wimsatt. The next available opening was that day at two, so Clare took it, deciding right then and there not to call Rod to tell him where she was going and really feeling good about that decision.

She drove down the empty four-lane Transcendental Boulevard past Tranquility Kindergarten. It was recess. The jungle gym was built by some famous architect to look like funny animals. There were kids on the elephant trunk slide and kids on the monkey monkey bars. There were boys with a puffer fish rubber ball in the grass and girls jumping a snake rope on the blacktop and a few unidentifiable little darlings just rolling in the dirt.

"CLARE," SAID DR. Wimsatt, "my receptionist told me you sounded a bit unsettled on the phone."

"No," said Claire. "I'm feeling very settled. It's just that my prescription has almost run out. I only have a few left. I *am* feeling unsettled about that. Maybe that's what your receptionist meant."

"But your dosage is at fifty-milligrams a day. You should have plenty. . . "

"Yes, well, that's what's so particularly unsettling,"

interrupted Clare, anxious to get to the story she had thought up to tell Dr. Wimsatt. "One of Rod's friends got into it. I think she used the medication *recreationally*. I wasn't going to tell you, but…"

"She?" Dr. Wimsatt was very perceptive. That was what Clare liked about her. That and her cheery office—the pink walls and the west-facing picture window.

"Yes," said Clare. "She. One of Rod's childhood friends. She lives in Colorado or Oregon, I think. Anyway, she was in the area and Rod invited her over for dinner. She's one of these 'free-spirit' types. Do you think I should have reported her to the police?"

"Clare, I want to phase out of that now and phase into the specifics of your married life."

"Oh, Rod's very committed. We're both very committed."

Dr. Wimsatt renewed her prescription on the condition that they schedule another appointment in two weeks to discuss how things were going, and Clare readily agreed.

It wasn't until she was driving back to Tranquility with her brand new bottle of Sobritol that it occurred to her that she hadn't remembered to take her birth control pill yet, and she wondered if it might be a good idea to stop taking it altogether without telling Rod. But she worried that an obstetrician might be able to find that kind of thing out. Or what if she did get away with it and Rod kept inviting women to dinner? They would go on drinking wine. Go on talking politics, naming countries she'd never heard of. And there she would be. There at the dinner table. Bloated and vomity. Full of whims and cravings.

"WHAT THE HELL is this?" Rod asked when he saw the I ♥ MY WIFE bumper sticker Clare had bought him at the gas station on the way home.

"Just something for the Audi," she said.

"This is some fundamentalist thing."

"I'm sure anyone can have one if they want to."

Rod grabbed the sticker, pealed it from the wax paper backing and slapped it onto his chest. "Real passive-aggressive, Clare," he said. "Real deep-seated shit."

"You're ruining your shirt."

He wrinkled his chin at her.

"That Miss Kim wasn't wearing any panties, Rod. And she was all bald down there like she was pretending to be a little baby running around on the beach or something. Is that what men like? Woman-babies?" She was crying now. She didn't want to be, but she was. "Anyway," she said, "I thought Asians were supposed to be demure."

"Hey, I've got an idea," said Rod. "Let's get out the tape recorder. I'm dying for you to hear the way you twist things around."

The argument went the way arguments do. The purple from Rod's wrinkled chin spread out over his face and bald head.

He said he was just trying to find her a friend or two because she was too socially retarded to do it herself. She wondered aloud why all these new friends he was finding her had to be so sexy— why he never seemed to find her an ugly one, or how about a nice couple? How about that? He asked if she was accusing him of something, if she really wanted to go there. She said why shouldn't she? She was his wife, why shouldn't she go there?

Then he was out in the yard, shouting out to the construction workers, "I love my wife! I love my jealous, fundamentalist, social-retard wife!"

Clare hid behind the potted palm in the living room, wanting to knock him off that high horse he was always riding around. *Clop, clop* at work selling copy machines. *Clop, clop* meeting women on his way home. *Clop* in the kitchen with his six o'clock vodka tonic, and *clop* let's enjoy being married awhile, and oh my aching back and *clop, clop, clop* into the bedroom to change.

Rod had stopped yelling now and was just standing there, maybe waiting for a laugh or an echo or just being philosophical about their marriage while the purple drained out of his head.

All day long Clare had been trying hard not to think of what might have happened last night between Rod and Judy Kim. Now she did think of it. Now she couldn't seem help herself. But you never knew with thinking. Where it might take you. And it was out of this very thought she didn't want to think that a plan came to her. A really good plan.

Clare went to it right away: When Rod came back into the house, she told him she was sorry, that she had been unfair and wrong not to trust him. Then she suggested that tomorrow night they should have that girl come over for dinner. "You know," she said. "The small one? Mickey? Why don't you call her up right now and ask?"

"FOR IDEAL TENDERNESS and flavor," read the recipe for roast duck with red cabbage and shitake mushrooms, "let stand at low for ten minutes after cooking time. No more, no less!"

Mickey was set to arrive at 5:30, and they usually ate dinner around six. So Clare put the duck in the oven at 2:50, wanting the timing to be just right. Then she treated herself to an herbal essence bath, made up a list of eight conversational questions to ask Mickey, memorized the list, buried the list in the kitchen trash, set the dining room table, washed the more visible windows, dusted, decided against cleaning the bedroom, emptied the twelve capsules of Sobritol from the old bottle into the smallest of her nesting bowls for easy access, threw the shells down the garbage disposal, did a trial run in which she poured a bit of the Sobritol into a vodka tonic and stirred just to make sure the powder would disappear, made a spinach salad, and had an hour left for clothes and makeup.

At 5:20 she sat back in the easy chair wearing a baby blue

double slip dress and pumps.

At 5:33 the duck was already done, and Clare turned the oven down to low.

At 5:42 she considered taking a little Sobritol herself and at 5:47 decided against it.

At 6:01 she wandered into the room that would someday be the baby's. It was empty. Clare had wanted to decorate it when she was doing the rest of the house, but Rod had teased her about whether it would be pink or blue and then become annoyed when she had suggested yellow.

Clare must have been very involved with that memory not to have heard Rod come in. "Look what I found wandering around outside!" he said, startling her. Mickey stood next to him in the kind of outfit that some people might say was just asking for trouble—a top so scant it might have been a handkerchief, no bra, a short pleated skirt and open-toed heels with laces that crisscrossed up her ankles and lower calves. Wanting to be as friendly as possible, Clare kissed the young thing on either cheek as if the two of them were European.

Then she ushered her husband and the girl into the living room and told them it would be her pleasure to prepare the drinks. Two vodka tonics coming right up. Clare poured a bit of the Sobritol powder into Mickey's and a bit more into Rod's. Not too much, though. The trick, she decided, was to do the thing gradually, so that the drug's effects would just seem like drunkenness until it was too late.

"Oh, thanks?" Mickey said when Clare brought the drinks out. And then, "What's that smell?"

"That smell is roast duck with red cabbage and shitake mushrooms," Clare said.

"Um, sorry, I can't eat that? I just started a diet where I get in touch with my body? And right now it's telling me I can't eat anything with pain nerves?"

"Maybe you can just have bread and spinach salad," Clare suggested.

Mickey put her drink down on the coffee table. She folded her hands and closed her eyes. "My body needs . . . My body needs"—a squeak came from the back of her throat—"tee . . . tee . . . toaster waffles? Do you have toaster waffles?"

"We have whole grain toaster waffles."

"Whole grain is good," said Mickey. She looked out the window and then at Rod. "Could we eat outside in that housey, bird-cagey thing?"

"You mean the gazebo," Rod said.

"Yeah. That. I mean, if it's not any trouble, but wouldn't that be cool?"

Clare started to say that the dining room table was already set, but Rod interrupted her.

"No trouble," he said.

Clare tried to smile as she reminded Rod that he didn't

like to eat out there. "Honey," she said, "Rod? Remember?"

"Just tonight," he said. "It'll be cool."

Clare could feel a hot panic starting to rise. Had they eaten dinner inside as she'd planned there would have been no problem. They could enjoy the duck she'd made even if the tenderness and flavor were not absolutely ideal and then pass out maybe sometime around dessert. But if Rod and Mickey passed out in the gazebo someone might see—a neighbor or a construction worker.

"I'm gonna get changed," Rod said.

"Here, take your drink."

Rod took the drink and headed down the hallway toward the bedroom. "Get to know one another!" he shouted back. "But no baby talk, all right?"

"Why don't we set the table?" Clare suggested. "I'll get a tablecloth." She made for the kitchen, where she hurriedly mixed two more drinks and then stood looking into the bowl of Sobritol powder. There was no way of knowing how much it would take to put the two of them out in the next short while, and, then again, too much could probably kill them. And how long could she hold out on dinner? One more drink? Two? Should she abandon the plan altogether? What kind of half-baked plan was this, anyway?

"Uh, Clare?" she heard Mickey say from outside the swinging kitchen door.

Clare left the drinks on the counter. Mickey was waiting

for her with a stack of plates and utensils gathered from the dining room table.

Clare led the young thing outside. She decided to be casual, conversational. She started in on her list of questions. "Is Mickey short for something? Michelle maybe?"

"No, just Mickey? My parents were eccentric a little?"

Mickey accidentally bumped one of the plates with a fork she was setting next to it, a quick little stumble; Clare told herself not to jump to conclusions.

"Do you have a boyfriend, Mickey?" she asked.

It was 7:17. The sun was still high, the construction workers still out there.

"No. Guys just like me for my body or whatever? Cause I'm so thin? But I can't find anyone who likes me for me?"

"I'm sure."

"Like I think Rod really appreciates women? Like for our inner courage and how we can have babies and stuff? . . . Oh. Sorry. Babies . . . But like he's good at compliments? I bet he just compliments you all day. You know what he said when I saw him outside? He said that if he was a woman he'd want to look just like me? Isn't that sweet? . . . Oh. Sorry. Was that? Sorry . . ." The young thing finished with the utensils and dashed inside.

After a moment Clare followed. There were only salad bowls and candles left to be brought out; Clare watched Mickey gather them up and scurry away.

In the kitchen, Clare dumped all the rest of the Sobritol into the drinks. But the powder didn't dissolve this time; it settled onto the bottom of the glasses. You could see it. She stirred. She stirred again. She was still stirring, furiously, a spoon in each hand, the drinks foaming up, when Rod came into the kitchen.

"Uh," he said. "You all right?"

"Fine, fine, here are more drinks." She handed them over, decided to risk it. She said she was a little anxious was all. She just wanted everything to be perfect, she said, and then they were late and she wasn't sure if the duck would turn out.

"It's fine," Rod said. "Clare. It's fine." And then he was gone.

Clare tossed the salad as quietly as possible so that she could listen to what went on in the other room. Rod was telling Mickey about his weakness for movies about animals. "I'm a real sucker for the ones about the dog trying to find his way home," he said. Clare heard a glass being set down on the coffee table every forty-five seconds or so. That would be Rod's. Mickey, the wife had noticed, held hers in her lap.

It was 7:26 and she didn't even dare look at what kind of shape the duck was in.

To take her mind off things, she decided to organize the spices alphabetically. Allspice . . . Bay leaves . . . Coriander . . . Cumin . . . It was 7:37 . . .

"When we eating?" Rod called out.

"Why don't I open a bottle of wine?" Clare called back. "All right."

Clare poured two more capsules into Mickey's glass and four more into Rod's— capsules from the new bottle, the bottle she'd been meaning to keep all to herself.

She brought out the wine and took away their vodka tonics. And weren't they slurring a bit? Just a little? Didn't they grab at the wineglasses a little sloppily?

Clare finished with the spices and was pacing the kitchen. How many capsules was that in all? she wondered. Let's see . . . twelve and then another six, so eighteen . . . maybe ten for Rod and eight for Mickey . . .

The vegetable drawer. She could organize it into two alphabetical rows—arugula . . . basil . . . cabbage . . . carrots . . . onions . . . shallots . . . shitake mushrooms . . .

That's when she heard it. Unmistakably. The thump and ring of a crystal wineglass hitting the carpet.

Rod was sliding off the sofa with his eyes closed and a dreamy smile that made Clare want to give him a smack in the face. Mickey slumped with her head between her legs. Her wineglass lay on the floor, the Merlot seeping into the brand new carpet.

"Whoa," the young thing said from between her legs. "Whooaaa."

For just a moment, Clare felt a maternal pity for her. But this was not the time for that kind of thing. So she went to get the *Zap-Gone Oxidizing Cleaner* she had ordered off the Home Shopping Network last month, and when she returned both Rod and Mickey were entirely out. The cleaner worked every bit as wonderfully as advertised, leaving behind only a clear, fresh, wet spot in the place where the wine stain had been. "Zap-gone," Clare said out loud, giving a squirt in Mickey's direction.

She checked both their pulses to make sure everything was all right in that department. Then she took her unconscious husband by the legs and dragged him into the bedroom like she had seen them do with dead people in the kind of movies she didn't like. She propped his legs up on the bed and crouched down on all fours to nudge the rest of him up. But his body was so relaxed it was like trying to maneuver a hundred and sixty-two pounds of dough; it kept sagging at odd places. Clare was no quitter, though, and after some hard thinking, she came up with the idea of using the ironing board as a ramp.

The folder of baby portraits fell onto the floor when she went to retrieve it, but Clare decided to leave it there for now and concentrate on the task at hand.

The task at hand was difficult and more than a little dangerous; Clare almost dropped her husband three times; the ironing board was bending, and she knew that if Rod woke up it would be tough to explain exactly what was going on. Finally, though, it worked. And after undressing him she went to get Mickey, who was so light that Clare could carry her to bed like you might a baby or a bride.

She unlaced and removed first the right heel and then the left, revealing a pair of the loveliest little feet she had ever seen—like two curvy, sexy little creatures themselves. Of course she would have nice feet, Clare thought. Of course she would. Mickey's top was tied in a bow at the back. Clare looked toward Rod. She picked up his arm and let it fall. His face didn't even twitch. The young thing's top came off with one quick pull and her skirt soon followed. Clare had to close her eyes as she tugged the girl's panties off, and when she opened them again to yet another bald private region she couldn't help feeling there was some sort of conspiracy going on.

She bundled up Rod's shorts next to his pillow. She hung Mickey's top from the upper left bedpost and placed her high heels on either side of the bed with the laces tangled. She tried to think of this as a kind of art project. Rod's shirt from yesterday with the I ♥ MY WIFE sticker was sitting on the golden oak dresser, and Clare's real moment of inspiration came when she decided to hang it over a drawer so that he would see it immediately after awakening with the young thing.

She positioned them spooning at first, but their bodies kept sliding apart. So eventually she had to give up on that and instead positioned Rod straight on his back with Mickey's head on his chest and her arm across it.

BY 8:16 CLARE was out in the gazebo enjoying a glass of iced tea, a duck breast and some spinach salad. The sun was just beginning to set, lighting the surface of New Walden Pond in a warm red. A last construction worker was loading what looked like a wooden box into the bed of his truck. She gave him a spirited wave and he gave one back. The duck breast was ideally tender and flavorful, despite what the recipe had said. Clare had picked up the folder of baby portraits off the closet floor and was flipping through them as she ate.

One thing at a time, she'd told herself when she had first come up with the plan. Now that she had them unconscious in bed together she would have to think up some kind of story that involved her leaving for the night. Some kind of emergency, she would say. A friend in need. An old friend. No one Rod knew. Didn't he remember when she left? Had he been too drunk to remember *anything?* (Not that she really would leave the house, of course. No, she would be on the couch, a light sleep, a few hours and then up to listen and to wait.)

And anyway, her explanation, whatever it ended up being, would come much later, after his. After she walked in and found the two of them in bed together. And then . . . And then . . . Well, then he would be sorry, wouldn't he?

Clare wasn't going through the baby portraits with any real purpose. They were just something to put her eyes on at while her mind ran in other directions. She wasn't looking for anything, but she found it anyway. Only a few portraits from the last. One of the earliest she had drawn. There was something about that one. And suddenly Clare knew—the way a woman can know a thing.

It was a girl. Fair skin. Sharp eyebrows. "Small mouth= secrets (me)." And even her feet would be her mother's.

SIX MONTHS IN, ANOTHER KIND OF UNDRESSING

SHE WANTS TO have sex, but it's only a one-bedroom apartment, and her toddler's asleep in the dirty white chair next to the bed.

"What if he wakes up?" I ask.

"He's not gonna wake up."

"Yeah, but what if he does?"

"He won't. Fuck, what if he does? He's seen worse shit."

"It's not . . . I can't . . . I think this is an issue of cultural differences."

We compromise on sex in the kitchen. So added to all the other things I'm already trying to ignore is the smell of milk and beer gone bad, and the line of ants traversing the brown grime that coats linoleum floor. Still, she herself is an easy distraction, a slender, twenty-one-year-old Latin Snow White who flutters het eyes innocently even as her body does otherwise.

Up until now, she would appear at my apartment a few nights a week in tiny shorts and high, high-heels, throw down a couple beers before we got to it. Dirty stuff, and loud. Epiphanies of deviance and skin. This is the first time she's invited me to her place, invited me to meet her toddler, and only briefly have I allowed myself to wonder why. He and I played awhile before he fell asleep. House. We played house.

Not so long ago, when she herself was a toddler, she would listen to baseball on the radio with her grandpa, even though she'd never seen a game and didn't understand what "runs," what "steals," what "home" even meant. Once, he'd let her crayon his white hair rainbow just because she wanted to. Later, he couldn't wash the waxy rainbow out. Had to shave his head. When she was twelve, he died, the first of many men to let her down.

I'm going to leave this country soon. In her building's rotting stairwell, as I say the small goodbye that only hints at the bigger one, she sobs and grabs and pleads love, though all she's pleaded until now is fucking. And, I, thirty-two, polite behind my glasses, convince both her and myself that I'm surprised.

The building is dim, the ceiling low. The neighbor with the moustache and gym shorts watches from his doorway as if we're something on Telemundo.

Our noise wakes up her son. He runs into the hallway. Chuckles, squeals, makes a jumping lap around us, trying his little-boy best to make Mom happy again. He does her favorite game, the one she's always trying to get him to do in front of her friends—his Elmo dance, his Elmo dance for her.

UGLY AROUND HIM

THE BUS DUMPS Masky and his fat wife at the corner, and Cleburn Street pulls them down its slope toward home. It's summer. Clouds spread low like an extra ceiling the trees are holding up. Masky's fat wife's got her arms around a tub of Kentucky Fried Chicken. She made them get off the bus from the hospital to get it and then they had to wait half an hour for another one.

The houses on Cleburn Street are old wood or new stucco or trailers, some of them, each on its own lawn with Martian weeds and brown spots. Some have walls that spill rocks and concrete onto where a sidewalk should go. Masky's walking in front of his fat wife so he won't smell the chicken as much.

There's no one else outside except Ed Hold, the sex offender, pushing his manual mower over the lawn he keeps so nice. His garage door's open; his '79 Firebird's poking its hood out. He's wearing a cap that says, "If I'm such a baby, feed me," with the *e*'s from "feed" shaped into breasts. He's thirty-four,

121

six-three, two hundred and seventeen pounds, and if this day made shadows, his would reach out over Masky and the fat wife both. Ed Hold stops mowing when they go by. He pulls his cap down over his heart and stands watching them like he's saying the Pledge of Allegiance, except that he's not. His face is flat with no look there—just a mouth stretched tight between two rosy cheeks, so it's hard to tell what he means by standing like that, though Masky's pretty sure it's mockery.

GRACE, HIS FAT wife's named, but she's never said grace until now—knees in the carpet, head over dinner, eyes not even shut. Grace saying grace and looking at chicken.

Masky's sitting across from her drinking Jim Beam, watching her chin go triple and more while she mouths whatever she's mouthing.

Then Grace says, "A-men," and grunts herself up. She gets her teeth in a chicken thigh. He hears her swallow, hears wet, ripping sounds as she pulls the chicken joints apart. Masky's not hungry; he's just having Jim Beam for now.

"I ain't goin' in cars no more," Grace tells him for maybe the fourth or fifth time.

It had been a red '93 Buick Regal or else a '94 that had hit their girl. Masky didn't see it happen and by the time he got outside, the Regal was turning off Cleburn onto Highway 71, so it was hard to tell exactly.

His girl, though—her year was '96. She was eight.

An ambulance came. Masky and Grace rode along. That was yesterday.

Today when the body was wheeled out, Masky's fat wife's fat family was there saying no one should be alone right now. Saying they'd all come over to the house: bring the flowers and cards from the hospital room, bring secret family recipe casseroles, bring more fat people with more things to say. "The fuck you will," Masky told them. And that's when Grace had first started in about no more cars. Like it was revenge on him.

"You gonna ride the bus your whole life?" he asks her now.

She chews. She swallows. "Yeah," she says.

The phone's off the hook. The door to his girl's room is shut. There are crayons and juice stains and naked Barbies on the floor. Sympathy cards on the window ledges and the top of the TV say things like, "Words fail to express the great sadness that has befallen, but please know you have a friend in me." They're all from people Grace knows—her family and such. She brought them home in her purse and set them up first thing.

Masky's glass of Jim Beam's empty. Grace always says it's tacky to have the bottle on the table with dinner and she won't let him do it—not even when his girl gets killed by a Buick Regal she won't—so now he's got to go to the kitchen for more. On the refrigerator there's a crayon drawing his girl did. It's of a snowman thing with cherries for earrings. The thing's name is Wolfy, even though it doesn't look like a wolf. Wolfy used to be the monster in the closet until his girl decided that they should be friends.

Masky takes the picture off the refrigerator and puts it in a drawer, but not before noticing another picture drawn on the back. This one's of the emblem on the hood of Ed Hold's Firebird. Masky had caught her once at the mouth of that garage. He'd pulled her away saying never, never, never, never, never.

Grace and he had talked about moving someplace else then, but didn't want to spend their girl's college fund to do it. None of that matters now anyway.

There isn't much Jim Beam left and wasn't much to start. Masky pours it all into his glass. "How 'bout the funeral?" he yells from the kitchen. "You gonna ride a bus to your own girl's funeral?"

She doesn't answer or he doesn't hear her. And when he gets back to the table she's crying and eating like the wet makes it go down easier.

Masky sits in his chair across from her. He's not hungry; he's just having Jim Beam for now.

GRACE, SHE'S NAMED, but she doesn't have any. Slow and sleeping-pilled, she unbuttons her blouse like she just learned how, asking do they make coffins in blue. Four rolls of fat hang over her hips, but her legs are skinny, stolen from the woman she used to be before she got pregnant and kept the weight. Now she's built to fall. And when she steps out of one pant leg then the other it looks to Masky, watching from bed, like she will.

Her weight tips forward. Her back leg kicks out wiggling into the air like it's looking in the wrong place for the floor. A still second, maybe half of one, before she catches herself and scoots into the bathroom.

Masky shuts his eyes. He hears the water running over Grace and down the drain. He's hoping he'll be asleep before her shower's over and she comes back to bed. He figures his chances are good since last night he didn't sleep at all. He'd been up with his girl. Watching her like watching a baseball hooking foul, thinking if you do it hard enough it'll go your way. He watched her so hard he forgot the woman next to him was his wife or that he had a wife at all. And so hard he didn't even notice the doctors and nurses until the middle of the night when he had to buzz one. "Hook me into a piss bag like the one you got her on," he said, careful not to move his eyes from his girl.

The nurse said she couldn't do that.

"I got insurance," he told her, "I got money," thinking of the college fund.

The nurse said no again, and Masky tried to grab her arm, but got her thigh instead. There was a lot of noise—Grace crying and the nurse saying something about dignity. "Shhh," Masky had told them. "Shhh," for his girl, hooked up to all those bags and machines and looking like something you see on a show exploring the deepest parts of the ocean. All just skin and breathing.

Masky's dreaming that and remembering it, too. Then he dreams and remembers Ed Hold mocking him this afternoon. So when he dreams about walking over to the sex offender's house and picking up the manual mower with the superhuman strength moms get to lift station wagons off their babies and bringing it down on Ed Hold's skull, that seems like a memory too. And it feels good to do that. To be that kind of man.

Masky hears a crack. That crack is three things at one time: the mower smashing Ed Hold's skull, the Buick Regal smashing his girl's body, and the cracking of his fat wife's ankles as she moves back into the bedroom. Masky keeps his eyes shut. Grace kneels against the bed to pray more. Then she starts crying in a squeaky way that he knows is supposed to wake him up, but he keeps his eyes shut still. He even keeps them shut when she turns off the light and gets into bed and scoots close to take comfort from him with her hot, fat arms.

—BUT NOW HE can't sleep and his fat wife took the last two pills. So he's standing on the kitchen counter to see if there's anything else to drink up in the high cupboards. The high cupboards are where they keep all the disasters that never happened: Draino, plastic shopping bags, exacto knives, matches, liquor, the Sex Offender Information Bulletin about Ed Hold. Masky digs a half pint of something out from behind a glass statue of a swan with the beak too sharp. There are raspberries on the label. It tastes sweet like it's made for kids. It twists his stomach.

He climbs down from the counter with the half pint and the Information Bulletin. He opens the refrigerator for the bucket of chicken. Takes the lid off and looks inside at patches of grease gone solid and places where bones poke out.

He can't eat, so he calls the number on the Sex Offender Information Bulletin. "I got an inquiry," he says. "Subject's full name is Edward Edwin Hold at . . ."

"Is this Mr. Masky?" the lady interrupts. "How are you, sir? How's your girl?"

"Says here, it says, 'level three sex offender,'" Masky continues like she hasn't said anything, "How many levels they got?"

"Still three, sir. I'll be sure to call you if anything changes." She sounds like she's doing something else while talking to him. Maybe her nails or solitaire.

"I got another inquiry," says Masky. "That girl he sexually offended. Could be she was temptating him on purpose."

"We generally don't blame the victim, Mr. Masky."

"Yeah, okay. But females temptate sometimes. You know that, they sometimes do."

"Mr. Masky, my detective's intuition's giving me the

feeling you want to tell me something."

"Lady, you're wrong," says Masky, then hangs up the phone and holds it down hard awhile before taking it off the hook again.

Masky didn't used to have trouble sleeping. It came along with his girl. In '96. He'd sit up and drink and worry about Ed Hold or the disasters in the high kitchen cupboards or the way his girl ripped the clothes off her Barbies or what might happen if his girl got fat and boys didn't like her. Or if she stayed pretty and they did.

Sometimes Masky would call that lady detective on the Sex Offender Information hotline and ask her all kinds of questions trying to figure out how dangerous Ed Hold was. He imagines that lady detective now as someone who wears red lipstick and no panties and works this job because she secretly gets excited about sex offenders. He wants to call her back and say he knows these things. But he doesn't do it.

The Maskys don't get cable TV and the only magazines there are about how to raise your kid, so all he can find to masturbate to is the weatherwoman on channel thirteen. She's wearing one of those skirt suits.

High-pressure, she says.

THE CLOUDS HAVE come down over the low trees now and Masky's got to duck. He's huffing up Cleburn Street toward Ed

Hold's house with the bucket of Kentucky Fried Chicken. The half pint of raspberry something's gone and he couldn't find anything else to drink.

He thought there'd be blood or skin or something gray and awful in the part of the street where his girl got hit, but there isn't. This part of the street looks the same as any other.

He goes past it. To the sex offender's house, where the blinds are down and light leaks around them. And now Masky's yelling.

Back before he'd gotten married and stuck in Fayetteville, before he had a fat wife and a normal-type job and a cheap Korean car so he could save up money for his girl, who liked bread with sugar on it and every kind of blue, Masky used to sell liquid soap to automatic car washes all over the tri-state region of Arkansas, Texas and Oklahoma. They used to get him a new Ford every two years for that job. Any kind he wanted. He'd climb out of that Ford and say to the gas station attendant or some other guy in some other Ford, "Gotta shoot on over to Bald Knob." "Shoot on down to Lott."

And so now when he runs out of things to yell about Ed Hold's rosy faggot cheeks and cracking his skull open with the manual lawnmower, Masky hears himself yelling about those Fords he used to drive.

Ed Hold's front door opens. He's there in front of its light like a shadow standing up. Then gone; the door's shut and it's dark. Masky's thinking the man has gone back inside, but he's wrong. And now Ed Hold's got him. The bucket of Kentucky Fried Chicken bumps the ground and the pieces rattle inside. Masky's confused; he can't tell the clouds from the concrete. There's hard breathing. And it feels like a long time before Masky knows he's not getting stabbed in the face or sexually offended; he's getting hugged. Ed Hold's mouth is close to Masky's ear.

"Neighbor," he's saying, "my sympathies concerning your daughter."

INSIDE ED HOLD'S house is a black mat to wipe your feet on. And a flowered couch and a painting of trees on the wall across from it where a TV would go. All the rest is plain empty white.

"What kind of condition's she in?" Ed Hold asks about Masky's girl.

"Dead condition," says Masky.

Ed Hold takes off his cap and looks at it there in his hands. Then he says, "So I guess we'll have the good stuff," and goes into the kitchen.

Masky sits on the couch, puts the bucket of chicken on the floor. He didn't know he'd say that—dead condition. The overhead light eats x-rays into him.

Ed Hold comes back with a fifth of Johnny Walker Blue and hands it right over—no glasses, just the bottle. He sits on the couch next to Masky. "They apprehend the driver?"

"No." He's never had such good whiskey before. He

figures he'll buy some tomorrow, that a man whose girl got killed by a Buick Regal should have his own bottle of good whiskey. "Want some chicken?" he asks Ed Hold.

Ed Hold peels the round cardboard lid from the bucket of chicken with both his hands until he's holding it like a steering wheel. And he throws his voice up high. "I'm a la, la, lady," he says. "I do not know the proper way to operate a motor vehicle." He honks the chicken lid twice and pretends to check his lipstick in the rearview mirror.

Masky grips the bottle of Johnny Walker Blue by its neck while Ed Hold goes on: "I declare I have decided to take a turn down Cleburn Street for a shortcut in order that I might pick up some feminine products."

So Masky tells him, "I seen you mockin' me when I come home today. Pledge Allegiance mockin' me, cause you couldn't get my girl, pervert, but somebody did. You mock me more and I'll take this bottle and smash your god-shittin' head in."

The sex offender doesn't seem scared. He puts his eyes on Masky like Masky's just another place to put them. "Hats off's all I meant to articulate there. Neighbor, hats off to you."

They drink. They drink in that kind of quiet that can last awhile and get inside you. So Masky says, "My girl got killed by a red '93 Buick Regal, or else a '94," because it's all he can think of.

"'94," Ed tells him.

"It's hard to know for sure. They both got that spoiler rack."

"Neighbor, that was a '94."

Masky looks at the painting of trees awhile. Then he asks, "You seen it? You seen it happen?"

"Yeah."

"You sure it was a lady driving?"

"Tell you the truth I didn't see her exactly, but I like to think I can determine that by the manner of how they drive."

"What'd it look like?"

"When she got hit?"

"Yeah."

"You wanna know?"

"Yeah. No . . . What'd it look like?"

Ed seems like he's thinking. Then he says, "It looked like pretty turned to ugly fast."

They keep drinking and time gets lost, so that now Ed's saying about the painting of the trees where the TV would go, "For my serenity of mind. No people," and now he's on to something about diamonds. "You know they can manufacture perfect cubic zirconium diamonds which no expert, Neighbor, can tell from real genuine? But if you think the ladies are going for that, well, you're mistaking the case. The ladies want them real. They say"—he's back in his lady voice now—"'gimme the ones from Africa what the nigger kids get their hands cut off for.'" He passes the bottle. He goes back to his real voice. "The whole difficulty," he says eventually, "arose because she refused me fornication excepting when Jay Leno was on. Neighbor, I attempted compromise. I taped the program. But I could just lay there with my hard-on sticking into the air as far as what concerned her."

The chicken's on the floor between them. Ed hasn't had any. Masky's pretty sure that it's out of politeness, pretty sure that Ed won't have any until Masky does first.

"The daughter," Ed continues, "she was fourteen at that time. She was given, in my opinion, not enough guidelines."

"You got to give 'em guidelines," Masky says.

"Right, Neighbor, you do. I'd wager right now you gave your girl the best guidelines you had to give her. In fact, I'd like to take this opportunity to say your girl was never in danger of me ipso facto of that reason."

"I appreciate that," says Masky. And he does.

"But not this one," Ed says. "You've got to understand about this daughter. This daughter had no daddy to give her guidelines. This daughter was arriving home at one a.m. Sometimes two a.m., three, four, as late as five a.m. on some occasions. I would describe her choice of dress as of a provocative manner. For instance, to show her belly button wink at me. But I was the only one to see the problem there, you understand. Her mamma didn't have the proper clarity of vision to see it. And there was something else. An additional factor. Her clothes had this yanked appearance. Such as if they'd been pulled off and on her a great deal."

Ed stops. He grabs his cap from the couch and puts it back on. When he talks again it's under the cap's shadow and quiet. "I got her up against the refrigerator," he says.

Masky thinks Ed's going to go on talking, but he doesn't. So then Masky knows that in the way men are it's his turn to hand Ed the bottle. He does and Ed drinks.

And in a little while Masky feels that there's something of his own he'd like to admit, and that something starts with how good Grace's ass looked in jeans before she got pregnant and kept the weight. So he's talking about that, comparing that ass to different kinds of fruit and then an enchilada. He's saying that after the pregnancy it was like she kept that weight on purpose, like the good ass had already done its job and she didn't need it anymore. And all the while Ed is shaking his head slow like he understands exactly, like they aren't talking about women, but about some war they'd been in together.

So then Masky gets around to what he wants to say: "She's the one wanted a kid. Took that ass in jeans and waggled it. Hypnotose me. I didn't want no kid. The worry of it."

Ed's still shaking his head slow like that, communicating, yeah that's it. That's how it can be.

THEY TAKE THE whiskey and bucket of chicken out to the garage. Ed shows Masky the 220 hp, 400 cubic inch V8 engine on his '79 Firebird and explains how he cleans it with Q-tips. Ed shuts the hood. The red Firebird emblem has its wings spread around a deep front spoiler. "This one's a bottom breather," Ed says, "on account of the fact that the front grill on the earlier model's been replaced by an aerodynamic beak. So this one pulls up air from the bumper grills and under the front."

They move around back. "See the tail lights?" Ed says, "Their black appearance? They still illuminate red, but the way this car's built it's like it's got no brake lights, no breaks understand, because it's built to move. When it's not moving there's something wrong about it."

They climb inside. Masky's in the passenger seat. When he leans over to see how high the speedometer goes, Ed gives him a man's honest look. "We're buddies, right?" says Ed. "We confided?"

"Yeah."

"Well, buddy, if I was you in a time of need like you are, I'd have a lady on my boner."

"She's asleep."

"No, I don't mean that over there. I mean the good stuff. The stuff with no ugly on it. I know the location of a facility in Nevada."

"A whorehouse?"

"This is a special secret facility I know. These ladies can satisfy a man with their earlobes or even the blades of their shoulders."

"I got money," says Masky.

Ed hands over the bucket of chicken and the Johnny Walker Blue to Masky in the passenger seat and meanwhile he's talking about those ladies. "So good they're not human," he says, "Just money-operated . . . Containing no hair on their bodies . . . Tits they got, proportions such as is impossible . . . Such as if NASA constructed them."

He shuts his door. He buckles his seatbelt. "Take us a whole twenty-four hours to get there, but whoa it's gonna be worth it." He starts the engine and honks the horn. "The phoenix rises from the ashes!" he yells. He clicks the garage door opener and there's the sky in front of them.

It's low, but wide.

AND MASKY COULD be out under it now. He could. Johnny Walker Blue in his hand, bucket of Kentucky Fried Chicken in his lap for when he's ready to eat again. That Firebird moving like it was built to, sliding easy past the place his girl got hit by the '94 Buick Regal and up the slope of Cleburn Street like both were nothing. Turning onto Highway 71 and off to some location in Nevada where all the women take from you is money.

But then for some reason, he's not. For some reason, he told Ed thank you very much, but no. And now instead he's back home. Stumbling past his girl's shut door into the bedroom where his wife's asleep.

Instead he's stuck in his pants. He didn't take off his shoes before undressing, and now he's all tangled. Falling. "Grace," he whispers. "Grace."

KEENER

SOMEONE WAS KNOCKING on the door. A small, insistent sound like the dripping of a faucet.

"Come in!" Jack yelled from his spot on the couch, and a nervous guy edged through the door, duffel bag first, his other hand cradling a book entitled *Please Understand Me II*. This was Penny's brother, Keener, a gangly mouth breather with an Adam's apple big as a Red Delicious. Jack recognized him from various photographs. "Good to meet you, Keener," he lied without bothering to stand up or offer a handshake. "Don't you live in Texas?"

Keener didn't reply, only ran his glance over the tarps and paint trays to the single sky blue X Jack had rolled out on one of the walls that morning before he'd gotten his idea for the Boston Baked Payday and started in on the prototype. The glance roamed from there to the coffee table where lay the Payday picked clean of peanuts, the pile of Boston Baked Beans, half-ounce an of pot, and a waterbong Jack had built into volume

17 of a 1991 *Britannica Macropeadia of Knowledge in Depth* (Sonar—Tax Law).

Jack took a hit and offered one, but Keener shook his head. He still hadn't said anything. Just stood there. "Your sister's not home," Jack told him. "She didn't know you were coming, right? I mean, you must not have told her, cause she didn't tell me."

Keener opened his mouth to speak, and when he finally did, it was with a nervous hitch, a phantom rattle, as if the Red Delicious were really his heart cut loose to knock around down there in the dark. "I'm . . . on a journey," he said. "To find my lost artistic. Vision. I. Took a bus."

ENGAGEMENT HAD BROUGHT Jack to Poughkeepsie, New York and the breaking of that engagement had left him here. So he re-enrolled in college, got some student loans and developed a fascination with a junior in his Art History class who had the biggest facial features he'd ever seen. It wasn't the features themselves that fascinated him so much as all the shadows they cast. The shadows were always shifting, so the question not just of beauty versus ugliness, but even more fundamentally of what she looked like to begin with could only be answered provisionally. Instead of notes on the lecture, he took notes on Penny Havel, inventing a name for every one of her looks and tracking their occurrence over each class meeting. His notes on October second, for example, read:

1:00 Film noir heroine

1:17 Delacroix's "Orphan Girl in a Cemetery"

1:35 Crayon drawing of the Hamburglar by a seven-year-old with ADD

Here was one girl who looked like a hundred, and it made perfect sense to Jack that he, who couldn't seem to decide on anything, would be attracted to her. So he asked her out. He dated her. He found out she'd signed up for Art History because of a younger brother who liked to paint, that her parents were the rich, distant kind, and that for reasons having to do with this, she thrived on taking care of people. And when Jack failed out and lost his dorm room, she invited him to move into her second floor apartment. He commandeered two drawers, a closet, a side of the bed, and a spot on the couch next to a window that overlooked the street.

KEENER HAD STARTED off from home last week, going first to "power zones" in Arizona and North Carolina. He told them all about it at dinner, using terms like *soul search, destiny* and *self-dependence.* There was only so much of this talk Jack could listen to, so a lot of the time he tuned it out and just watched instead. The siblings didn't look that much alike, he decided, but their looks had a way of answering each other, tying the other's loose ends, so that a face at one time more mysterious, more deserving of study than the last four hundred years of Western art—a face well-worth failing for—seemed just a little less so now.

Keener had been in the bathroom when Penny got home. And the nearly finished prototype for the Boston Baked Payday didn't seem to make up for the fact that Jack still hadn't painted the living room. While Penny looked at that sky blue X, her disappointment expressed itself through small, piteous tremors erupting all over her face, each smoothed out before the next one hit. When Keener came out of the bathroom, she was surprised to see him, and cried what are called tears of joy, but in truth were probably more complicated than that.

"Jack," said Keener. "What do you do? I mean. Since you failed out."

"Part-time at the mall arcade."

"Jack, that's not all you do. That's not all he does, Keen."

"Right. The other thing I do is smoke a lot of pot."

"I told you, Keen. He's an independent idea man."

The siblings had made dinner together. And even with the baseball game on, Jack could hear her defending him in the other room. "Two months," she'd said about his panting or not painting living room, though it had been closer to three. "He's a slow starter is all." Now, she was prompting him to defend himself. "Jack, tell Keener some of your ideas."

"I'd like to hear them," said Keener. "I would."

"Sure, alright. Just this afternoon I got an idea for a self-help book for people addicted to self-help books. It's called *Just*

Sweat the Small Stuff . . ."

"What about that new painting, Keen?" Penny interrupted. "You were excited about that one."

". . . Then there's the line of bumper stickers," Jack continued, "Cashiers do it fast and friendly. Carpenters do it with wood. Fishermen do it with their flies down. Basketball, baseball, football players or whatever do it with balls . . ."

Penny ignored him. "How'd that painting go, Keen? The abstract?"

"It started okay," said Keener. "But now it. Just looks like wallpaper."

"Hey, you should paint our living room walls to look like wallpaper," said Jack, and added, "Spies do it undercover."

TESTS. THERE WERE always tests. Now that Jack wasn't in college, Penny administered them instead. And then as now, they seemed so relentless that he almost felt dared to fail. Painting the living room was one. And how he would handle Keener another. Even now, settling down to bed came another one: She told him for maybe the tenth time the story of the one girlfriend Keener had ever had way back in high school, and she expected Jack to be patient and sympathetic. So when Penny explained how the one girlfriend had become a born again virgin just before meeting Keener, Jack made thoughtful sounds in the back of his throat. And whatever humor he found in the part of the story where Keener walked in on the girl mounting the assistant coach of the water polo team, he suppressed. Jack even went as far as pretending to follow the straight, rudimentary line Penny drew from this single incident to every one of Keener's problems, including whatever artistic crisis he was in the midst of now as well as the fact that while cashiers, carpenters, fishermen, ballplayers, and spies all seemed to be doing it, her little brother never had.

"Some female attention is all he needs," Penny concluded simply, hopefully.

"Right," returned Jack, and, satisfied with his performance, started drifting off to sleep. But Penny wasn't done.

"I've been thinking," she said. "It might be a good idea to invite Amanda over for dinner to meet him."

"Amanda who?"

"Amanda, who you almost married?"

"Oh. Her."

"I mean, they have some things in common."

"You mean because she lives with her parents too?"

"She might like him."

That Keener was creepy-ugly and socially hopeless— these things didn't occur to Penny, or else she didn't let them. Her psyche was like an old English mansion in winter. Whatever rooms couldn't be kept warm and bright were boarded up. To go prying boards loose wasn't such a good idea if Jack wanted to get to sleep soon, so instead he took the roundabout approach of pointing out that Amanda was five years older than Keener.

"So? You're five years older than me."

Jack made a tired sigh. "Okay, but your wanting to hook up your brother with my ex-fiancé is a little bizarre."

"If you can think of someone else, we can talk about it."

Jack had to admit that he couldn't.

"You're still in touch, right?" she said, "You call her sometimes?"

Jack admitted that he did.

"It's just dinner. Could you at least think about it? For me?"

Jack said that he would and started right in. He was fairly sure of Penny's genuine desire to do what she could for her brother. Still, she'd always been jealous of Amanda, and this felt like yet another test: to get Amanda over here and see Jack interacting with her, to confirm some suspicion, prove some point.

As Jack moved closer to sleep, his subject slipped from whether he should invite Amanda over for dinner to Amanda herself. It was Jack's idea that Amanda looked like a cow. Not one of those grubby, overfed, hormoned things they use for U.S. beef, but a nicely proportioned Swiss dairy cow. Bovine in her sway and generous curvatures, bovine in her eyes that spoke of boundless trust misplaced. He'd told her that once, meant it as

Adam Prince

a comic sort of compliment, but instead of taking it that way she crawled under her Snoopy football blanket and threatened to drown herself in the toilet.

Amanda made odd, obscurely comic suicide threats. Drowning in the toilet, Chinese water torture, lead poisoning. It was impossible to know how seriously to take her even after she started cutting herself.

Amanda got giddy on summer fruit and Christmas. She used the edge of his desk to masturbate, one foot on the floor, the other straight-legged against the wall.

Amanda had dark red hair and the virgin/whore thing down.

JACK CALLED HER from the mall arcade. "Penny wants you to come over for dinner."

Amanda's end of the line was quiet.

"*I* want you to come over for dinner."

"I can't. I have my Weight Watcher's meeting."

"Skip it."

"It's not up to me, Jack, I've put myself in the hands of a greater power."

"I promise we won't neck in front of you or anything."

"The grandmaster's very protective of me, Jack. He doesn't like it when I don't show up. That's not his real title— grandmaster. It's a pet name. He's this little Argentinean man

146

who dresses like a sailor. I'm not saying I'm in *love* with the grandmaster, Jack, but if he asked me to marry him, I would."

Jack had offered Penny and Keener a deal, and they had agreed to it. If he could get Amanda over for dinner, Keener would paint the living room. The way Jack saw it, he was trading in one test for another more interesting one. He didn't bring up the purpose of the dinner to Amanda or even mention Keener at all. Instead, he lifted that line from Penny: "Could you at least think about it? For me?"

"It's not really my job to think about things for you anymore, Jack."

All the same he knew she'd do it. Something in her. A love of trouble or of him. It took just one time around the track on the new *NASCAR Raceway* game before Amanda called back.

Jack in turn called Penny and reminded her of the deal. Still, when he came home that night, the sky blue X remained untouched. "We were too busy getting ready," said Penny, dropping marigolds into a copper bowl of water for a centerpiece. She had her hair pulled back and wore a dress the color of pantyhose.

Keener's way of getting ready seemed to involve a lot of nervous squirming on the couch while he read a book called *I Can Manage Life: Making Decisions and Learning to Grow.* Penny had dressed him in Jack's clothes.

The muffler on Amanda's Honda Civic had broken almost

a year ago when she and Jack were still engaged. Clearly, it hadn't yet been fixed. Jack went to the window to watch her parallel park: the way she backed in at the wrong angle and refused to pull out to try again, but just went on making whatever tiny corrections she could. It took a full five minutes before she stopped the car half on the curb and emerged under the streetlight in a red velvet dress that gave her the look of an eighteenth century French street whore.

The dress was too small. Her generous breasts spilled over. And hugging her in the dining room, Jack felt the laces undone at the back and skin under that. Penny and Amanda hugged too, like a couple of adolescents forced to waltz. Keener stood back.

"Who're you?" asked Amanda.

"This is my brother, Keener," said Penny, covering over with a host's perfect cheer whatever surprise she must have felt at Amanda's not knowing. "He's a painter."

"Oh," said Amanda in that honeyed voice that always hid any kind of seriousness. "Let's see . . . Two boys. Two Girls. I get it." She glanced toward the door. Jack wondered if he could still hold Keener to his end of the deal if Amanda walked out. She didn't, though. She turned to Keener instead. "What kind of things do you paint?" But Penny's little brother was too nervous for it; the Red Delicious bobbed up and down as he tried to speak, while Amanda prompted, "Landscapes . . .? Abstracts . . .? Mmmm . . . naked ladies? I bet it's naked ladies."

"Living rooms," said Jack.

"Not really," said Penny. "He doesn't really."

"Oh, yeah," said Jack. "He doesn't."

Penny lit the candles, dimmed the lights, and seated them—Amanda directly across from Keener and at a diagonal to Jack.

They had Linguini with clam sauce. Amanda said it was worth seven points on Weight Watchers.

"Weight Watchers?" said Penny. "Amanda, that's ridiculous. You don't need to lose weight."

"I just do it to meet fat men," said Amanda, and then, looking pointedly at Jack, "The good-looking ones never work out. Now the grandmaster—he's not fat. We can't have a fat guy run the meetings. But he *used* to be fat and that's the important thing. He's still got that fat man's kindness. It hangs on them like the extra skin. Oh, this is good wine."

Penny grabbed hold of the wine compliment to lead them onto safer ground. She mentioned where she'd bought the wine and drew everyone's attention to the painting of a duck on the label. "It reminded me of the duck stamp," she said. "Every year they have a competition. If you win they put your painting on the stamp and you get a million dollars. Keener got second place last year. You don't get anything for second, but it's very prestigious, huh, Keen?"

Keener nodded without looking up from his plate.

And that safe ground opened up to more safe ground as the dinner went forward. Penny talked about her brother like he was someone half-mythical—a celebrity or dead. In between other topics of conversation, such as Jack's idea for a dystopian remake of *Cannonball Run* called *Drunk Drive-a-thon* or whether he could get away with opening an all-beef hotdog place called Anne's Franks, Penny squeezed in cute things Keener had done when he was younger and how brave she thought he was for traveling around the country. She was coaxing her brother, soothing him. And gradually, very gradually, Keener lifted his gaze from his plate, to the table, to the company in general, to Amanda in specific. Still, the only sound to escape him all through dinner was a mumble that preceded each of his many trips to the bathroom.

It wasn't until the strawberry pie had been served that Keener actually spoke. "Uh. Man. Duh," he said.

"Yeah?"

Keener took a sip of water and then of wine. Everyone waited. "I have trouble with confidence and . . . male identification," he finally said.

"I have nervous breakdowns," Amanda shot right back.

"Where you can't get out of bed?"

"Where I can't get off the floor. Jack stepped over me. Didn't you, Jack?"

"Yup," said Jack.

AN INTERNSHIP INVOLVING the chemical makeup of the bell pepper kept Penny at school most days from ten to six, during which time Keener occupied the spot on the couch that Jack had once considered his own. He read self-help and looked out the window as if to discover his lost artistic vision there.

"So I notice the living room's not painted yet," said Jack.

"I need to. Find inspiration."

"You just paint solid. It's just walls."

"To you. To you it's just walls."

Nights were even worse. Penny would come home from her work on the bell pepper to work on getting her brother to call Amanda, since somehow she'd managed to construe their mutual dysfunction and aggression toward Jack as genuine chemistry. On the subject of when Keener might be moving on to the next stop along his journey, both siblings were evasive.

Jack started requesting extra shifts at the arcade. When the shifts weren't enough, he took long drives out along route 9 or 44 that promised to take him to Albany, to Philadelphia, to Providence. And he drove by the house on LaGrange where Amanda lived with her parents.

One night while Penny and Keener were making dinner, Jack was digging among the piles of self-help on the coffee table to get to the *Macropeadia*, when he found a book called *Manwatchers: A Woman's Guide to Diagnosing the Dysfunctional Male*.

"Did you get her this?" he asked Keener.

"I'm not making any accusations, Jack," Keener said right back, and in his voice not the slightest tremble, the smallest hitch.

That night in bed, Penny told Jack that he shouldn't take the book personally; it was just a lot of female attention going to her brother's head.

"What female attention? You're the only female giving him attention."

Apparently not. Amanda had called to ask Keener to a movie on Thursday. Penny put her arms around Jack in the dark. "You said you wouldn't mind," she whispered. And then, "I've got my book club that night. So I wanted to ask if you could find something, too. I mean, just in case, since they can't really go back her parents' house."

JACK HAD TO work until ten on Thursday. He figured he'd take a drive after that or have a couple drinks with Downer from the soft pretzel place. But when Thursday at ten actually came around he found himself driving straight home to his spot on the couch and the *Macropeadia*.

Maybe it was that book about men that made him do it, or the bottle of Chianti and two glasses that Penny had set out that morning. But more than anything, it had to do with Amanda, who liked to give her own types of tests. She'd always sort of poke at Jack to see how far he'd go.

So Jack smoked and waited, and had a beer. At some point, he looked at the cover of *Manwatchers*. It was a bunch of men staring into the camera, each with a different diagnosis floating above his head: Something to Prove, Compulsive Masturbator, No Ambition, Lost. He fought an impulse to open the book and had another beer instead.

When he heard the cough of Amanda's broken muffler, he got up and made for the kitchen pantry.

He heard the front door open. The squeal of a corkscrew. The pull, the pop. They were in the kitchen.

"I like that shirt you're wearing," he heard Amanda say.

"Uh, thanks."

"I bought Jack that shirt."

"Oh."

"I wonder if your sister knows that . . ."

Jack heard steps. Their voices drifted away. He waited a few minutes before climbing out of the pantry.

"Where's Jack?" he heard.

"I think. He went somewhere."

"His car's here."

"Yeah. I think he'll be gone for awhile."

"Ah," said Amanda. Jack heard the bubbling suck of the *Macropeadia*. "You want some? You should have some."

And this time Keener didn't refuse. There was the sound

of the bong and a coughing fit that followed.

"Are they gonna get married?" asked Amanda.

"Maybe. I'm not sure."

"There're some things she should know if they are. I should probably write some kind of document."

"Like how he stepped over you?"

"Yeah, and some other things."

More hits from the *Macropeadia*, then Keener said, "I got Penny a book. I have it right here. Can I read a. Part to you? I'd like to."

"Sure."

There was the sound of flipping of pages. Then Keener said, "'For the lost man, a relationship is not a cooperative endeavor but a battle of wills, a game that puts off the real business of living and making decisions. He is so caught up in 'scoring points' against the woman he is with that the relationship as a whole is doomed to fail. This is a version of self-sabotage. And in this sense, at least, the lost man is addicted to loss. He often puts his hopes into careers he knows will fail, thus confirming the sense of himself as the noble hero who the world has turned against. And yet, for all of this, he is a hidden romantic, lost in the 'will be' that never comes.'"

"Will be that never comes,'" echoed Amanda. "That's good. I'll put that in my document as a quotation."

Jack slipped through the door, eased it shut, and crawled

out under the dining room table to peek into the living room.

Amanda was sitting in Jack's spot in knee socks and a short orange tennis skirt. Keener was turned to face her. A revving, nervous motion had taken over his hips, scooting him gradually closer to her. "I think you're a woman . . . of great beauty and strength," he said. "Hawk and dove combined."

"Is that from the book too?"

"No," he said. "It's from my heart."

"It isn't very good."

"Sorry," he said, but kept on revving. "I would never step over you. Like Jack did. I would get down on the floor. With you and. Not get up until you felt better."

"We could have a taco bar down on the floor," she said. "Or pizza. I'd take that too."

"Yeah. We could." He was whispering now. Revving and whispering. "My therapist says I need to take more chances. I was wondering. If you agree with him." His mouth couldn't have been more than a few inches from hers. "Because if you do. If you want me to—I will unloose the primal me."

"Oh, god," said Amanda, "Don't do that."

A pause then, while Keener took the rejection in. "I have to go to the bathroom now," he said, and pulled his gangly self up off the couch, spun around and ran for it. The bathroom door slammed shut.

Amanda strode into the dining room. Embroidered in

the lower right corner of her skirt was one of those Thanksgiving horns of plenty, though this was the middle of April. Jack came out from under the table, stood to greet her. She seemed not at all surprised. "I've seen you driving by my house," she said.

He held the door for her and the two of them went down the stairs and out to her car under the streetlight and a moon that was either full or almost. A garbage truck went by.

"Jeez, Jack," said Amanda, leaning against the driver's side door of her Civic, "quit it with the look."

"What look?"

"That glazed look where I can tell you want to feel me up. It was okay when we were together Jack, I liked it, but jeez."

"I wasn't even looking at your breasts," said Jack, though he did so now. "Right when you said that I was considering the implications of that horn of plenty thing. I was looking down. Not even in the direction of your breasts. That's a good three feet."

"That," she said, "is a *great* three feet."

It was more humor than kissing, Jack thought—dry humor. But when he slipped his hand under her skirt he found nothing dry about it. Dark humor, then. Dark humor under a moon that was either full or almost. And he must have been more stoned or drunk or giddy than he'd thought, because it wasn't even until Amanda started digging in her purse for the car keys that would allow them to take their humor into her backseat that it occurred to him what a terrible idea all of this was.

Jack pulled away. He rearranged. He looked up and down the street.

Amanda had gotten into her car in the meantime and started the engine.

"You okay?" he asked.

"Fine," she told him, before bumping the SUV in front of her and setting off its alarm.

Jack hurried inside.

Keener was lying on the couch with his eyes closed. Jack considered doing some kind of test to see if he was faking, maybe pretending to punch him in the face. But he wasn't sure it would work, and then what if it did? What if Keener *was* faking? What if he'd seen the whole thing? What could Jack do about it?

So he got into bed. And the next thing he knew Penny's face was searching his in the dark. How did it go? Did he know anything? Why was Keener sleeping with his clothes on and no blanket? Jack tried to think. He could feel his brain grinding at it. "We'll see," he said eventually.

IT'S MORNING NOW and they have seen. Keener's gone. Off to Albany, to Philadelphia, to Providence, or maybe just back home. He's taken his duffel bag full of self-help books and left only *Manwatchers*. He's painted the living room—or, he hasn't so much painted the living room as done a painting on the wall opposite the giant X, a painting all in sky blue.

"Paint over it," says Penny.

But the painting is good. It's really good. "You've got to hand it to him," says Jack, but Penny isn't about to hand anything to anyone.

So in a tone befitting the gravity of the situation, Jack starts telling her the story of how this painting came to be.

"Paint over it," she tells him. She woke Jack up saying that and it's all she's said since.

What makes this painting so good isn't just the realism of the figures and the car or that it's done in these thin jagged lines. (They don't have any paint brushes nearly that small, and Jack interrupts his story to ask, "What do you think he used to get the paint on? Chopsticks?") But what really makes the painting good is the yearning, the need. Not from the woman against the car or from the man who's pinned her there, but from the painter. You can see the jealousy. Can see the painter's conviction that just to be able to do a thing like that with a woman would be purpose enough in life. Jack's not sure how all these emotions got packed into this painting, but there they are. Or else, he's pretty sure they are. He could be over-reading, and he'd like to ask Penny's opinion, but obviously that's out of the question.

"Paint over it," she says. She's standing with her back to the painting and her arms crossed. The trays, the cans, the rollers, the tarps are next to her in a pile.

Jack's in his spot on the couch. He's trying to explain. He

just got to the part of the story where the garbage truck passed. He was about to say that it was more humor than kissing, but with a little help from the *Macropeadia* has since thought better of it.

"Paint over it," says Penny. The shadows all over her face look like a Rorschach inkblot test, with dark, condemning diagnoses in each new read.

The story's almost over. He'd thought there was more to it, that it was longer and more complex, but it's seeming simple now and short. He's trying to stretch it out as far as he can. As far as it will go. Because while he's talking he's waiting, too. They both are. To see what he might do.

BRUISES AND BABY TEETH

THE FUNERAL SERVICE was an odd, disorienting experience, in which Marilyn was described in terms Walt would never have thought could apply: *gregarious*, they said, *devoted*.

It was odd that Walt had been invited, odd that the man with thinning hair and a pregnant wife could be Marilyn's son, odd somehow that Marilyn had died at all. A man's wife leaves him one day for her ice skating instructor, and he never hears from her again, until, more than thirty years later, he gets an announcement in the mail saying her funeral will be held at a cathedral in midtown Manhattan and that donations to the Breast Cancer Research Foundation will be accepted in lieu of flowers.

In the coat pocket of his new black and grey pinstriped suit, Walt carried one of the many things that Marilyn had left behind, a bundle of her baby teeth. All twenty. He thought it might be a nice gesture to give them to the ice skating instructor, who was not, as it turned out, the dashing, insidious, long-fingered

Frenchman he'd been imagining all these years, but short, hairy, and deeply sad.

Walt introduced himself at the very beginning of the reception, which took place in the cathedral's atrium, where the ground was wet from an early fall rain.

"Huh . . . Wow . . . Well . . . Walter," the ice skating instructor said. "Thank you for coming. All the way out from California, is that right?" The man was so obviously startled that Walt began to suspect the funeral announcement had been sent by mistake. Someone else must have been in charge of that, someone to whom "Walter Threw" was just another name in Marilyn Pomeroy's address book. Still, it was understandable, and Walt didn't mind. Not really.

"Yep," he answered. "Still living in the same old place. Too much house for a single guy, but I never saw any reason to move." Then in a lowered voice, he added, "Hey listen. I just want to let you know that there aren't any hard feelings about what happened all those years ago."

It was meant as a lead-up to giving the man the baby teeth, but it only seemed to further startle him. He squinted at Walt and made one of those preemptory, stalling, throat-clearing noises that indicated he had something to say but was thinking through the wording. The moment hung awhile. Then the other mourners crowded in, ending the conversation there.

Walt then considered giving the baby teeth to Marilyn's son

David, since he was soon going to have a baby himself. *Thought she might like it if you had these*, he imagined saying. *I've always found them a bit morbid myself, but she liked them, and anyway, it's important, isn't it? Family history? Passing things on?* But David was surrounded by mourners, too, and Walt decided to leave it for later.

He could have used a vodka then, but found some very passable red Zinfandel instead, and made a few friendly comments about the beauty of the service to people he didn't know. It was an enormous group of people. Five hundred easily. And yet he still hadn't recognized a single one. The aunts, the college roommates, all dead or far away.

He wandered over to the photographs from Marilyn's life that hung in chronological order along the atrium's ivied walls. Here was Marilyn the baby, Marilyn the preschooler, Marilyn the flutist in the high school band. The photos ended at one wall with her college days, then continued on at the next with her second marriage, so that in the place of her years with Walt was only an empty corner with the ivy sparse and the rough grey wall showing through.

Almost without thinking, Walt drew the bundle of teeth from his coat pocket and pulled apart the blue lace tie. He made a quick scan of the crowd to make sure no one was watching, then sprinkled the twenty teeth like seeds into the ground of that empty corner and stepped them down into it with his orthopedic shoes.

Walt Threw was fifty-nine and worked independently as a

middleman, brokering deals by introducing one person to another. More than intelligence or business acumen it was his ability to stand between, to fill spaces in an amiable way that had led to the acquisition of certain measured excesses—in wealth, in friends, in weight, in hope. Even now, he hoped. Hoped his new suit was thinning on him. Hoped still to run into someone he knew.

Indeed, it was just after this moment of pressing those teeth into the ground that Walt looked up to see a woman with light skin and delicate thinness making her way along the photos of that first wall. She wore a form-fitting dress that ran down her arms and up her neck. Walt recognized her, and a fit of goofiness took him: he stood photograph-still in the empty corner with his arm around an imaginary wife. "This is where I go," he announced when the woman came near.

Her eyebrows knit in panic as if she'd been caught doing something wrong. Walt thought she might run away. "Linda!" he said, "Linda Mallek. It's me. It's Walt. You were a bridesmaid at the wedding."

She laughed, a nervous, hiccupy thing that bit into the funeral quiet and drew attention from all around, so now she was blushing too.

Walt apologized and thought about how beautiful women had always made him act like an idiot. "You look great," he told her. "Exactly the same. How've you been? How've you *been*?"

There was a pause. She seemed to be thinking. "I don't

know," she said and started to cry. Walt hugged her. The dress was thin. The warmth of her skin pushed through.

LINDA DIDN'T CRY long. Soon she was telling Walt that she'd been out of touch for all these years, hadn't known Marilyn was remarried and living in New York until she'd seen the name in the obituaries just yesterday. And now she spoke in a calm, matter-of-fact way, as if the crying from moments before hadn't even happened.

In truth, Walt hardly knew her, but he was so generally interested in people that he tended to remember them well. She'd been Marilyn's "Little Sister" in the Big Sister program years before the couple had met. She was young at the wedding, maybe seventeen, one of those artistic types that always confounded him because it was hard to gauge what they wanted and thus hard to know how best to accommodate. But seeing her now was such gleeful relief—the familiarity, the direct line between this moment and that other so long ago. It was all much closer to what he'd imagined the funeral to be.

Soon the two were admiring those photos along the second wall, agreeing that Marilyn's face looked different from the one they'd known. "Happier," said Linda, "or sort of mischievous, like she's just about to tell this great, daring joke." This was the person described in those eulogies, Walt thought. The person he'd never known.

Linda stayed close, and soon Walt was lifting wineglasses

and prosciutto-wrapped artichokes off passing trays in pairs and introducing his companion to people he himself was only meeting for the first time: Marilyn's coworkers, her brother-in-law, the nurse at the children's hospital where she had volunteered.

"Are you still painting?" Walt asked Linda when they had a moment alone.

"You remember that?"

"Of course."

"That's so . . ." she said, looking for the word, "*decent* of you."

"Decent. I've always been that. Well, are you?"

"Still painting? A little."

"And . . . decent?"

"Well . . ." she said, flaring her eyes at him as she dipped down to sip the wine.

It was one of Marilyn's kooky little beliefs—and this memory came to Walt suddenly now—that each person's face resembled either a horse, a bird, a muffin, or some combination of two. If so, then Linda was the perfect bird. It wasn't just her face, either, but her body and way of using it. She was graceful but abrupt, had a nervous, darting quality, the way a perched bird will twitch into flight. It was as if she were talking herself into each single action: linger when you say *well*, sip the wine, give the glance.

As for Walt himself, he was all muffin: big face and wide,

inviting grin. He'd never been handsome, not even thirty years and fifty pounds ago, but his ability to put others at ease served him well with women, at least up to a point. Thus Linda and Walt's moment alone stretched into something longer. He told her the joke about the restaurant on the moon and followed with an anecdote of how his black lab Benny used to climb the avocado tree in the yard every morning to bite one off for breakfast. Eventually, the nervousness went out of her laugh, and her hand began to linger on his arm. So when she whispered that she'd like to go back to his hotel room now, he was only a little surprised.

Marilyn's son David and his pregnant wife were sitting on a nearby bench. It was a good opportunity for Walt to introduce himself, but he found that he no longer felt the need. He had nothing to give the young man now, and, at any rate, what would he say? I'm the man your mother left? Your name was my idea? I might have been your father, somebody's father, if only she'd let me? It all seemed too dark, too out of sorts with the gleeful upswing of his mood. Enough of this moping, he decided. Enough of this looking back.

IN THE HOTEL room with the light off, Walt ran his fingers through Linda's hair, kissed her neck, nibbled her ears, and all to little effect.

"You're so beautiful," he whispered.

"It's my skin," she said back in no whisper at all. "I try to stay out of the sun."

Walt took down her zipper, revealing lacy black underwear and a figure surprisingly shapely for its thinness. But she was so stiff, so unresponsive that he couldn't imagine why she had propositioned him in the first place. Aggravated and preoccupied, he mistook the dark patches along her hips and legs for shadows. But kissing his way down, he saw that they were bruises instead.

"I'm married," she told him, as if that explained it. "My husband's away. I took off the ring. My married name is Russell." And now she was suddenly, abruptly aroused, pulling his hands down to her hips, breathing heavily.

"I'm sorry," said Walt. "I can't. This is. It's just . . . ." But he didn't know what it was or how to say it.

This silence persisted as he walked Mrs. Russell back to her apartment—only the light tapping of her high heels, and from Walt's orthopedic shoes, no sound at all. He sensed she was angry with him, and he wanted to fix it, if he could only think of how. At some point she stopped in front of a sushi restaurant and mumbled something about how much she liked it, how often she ate there. Then in a clearer, more determined voice, "You *are* decent, Walt. That's something I remember thinking way back. I remember thinking that's a man who's going to take care of his wife." She shook his hand and left, skittering off across the street before he could even give her his card. He wanted to yell, call her back. Instead, he watched her step up to the opposite sidewalk, turn a corner, and disappear.

He walked back to his hotel blowing out bewildered sighs the whole way there. The next morning a plane carried him off from a hot fog around JFK and set him down in John Wayne Airport's clear and cheery brightness.

THE FRIDAY NIGHT after Walt's return, none of his friends were around. Family night, said Jack. Granddaughter's birthday party, said Darrell. Even the country club was quiet. Walt came home early, poured a vodka rocks and carried it from room to room, turning on the light when he entered and off again before he left. He wished Benny would follow like he used to, but the dog was old now and often kept to himself.

In the empty guest room, the room that might have been for a son or daughter had things worked out differently, Walt sat on the bed. His hand holding the tumbler of vodka looked old, and he thought of how young it used to look doing this exact same thing. "Vodker" Marilyn used to call it—for no reason, for silliness. She was quiet back then, but had a particular sense of humor, would use the word "cute" to describe a hamburger or a freeway overpass. Remembering all of this, Walt could almost feel again the intimacy during their first year of marriage. Like a couple of kids whispering conspiracies in a fort made from a cardboard box.

"Too much house for me," Walt said aloud and left that room, turned out the light.

He went downstairs and sat in his reclining den chair flipping channels for something that might occupy his attention. He'd been in this exact same chair watching *Three's Company* the night Marilyn announced she'd been cheating. Walt had sat without comment through an entire segment of commercials. He swallowed down a bit of vodka and with it a bit of the pain, so that when he finally did speak, his voice was level. He hazarded that maybe she didn't have enough to do to fill her time. He said that adultery seemed all the rage these days and even made a joke about the show. "Three's Company," he said. Then Marilyn went into the kitchen to stack dishes, clanking away in anger as if *he* were the one who'd done something wrong.

The next morning, Walt heard his wife's car start and he looked out the window to see her pulling away wearing only a nightgown. He ran downstairs, but she was already gone. He dropped into his den chair and cried. He considered going after her, what he would say—that she didn't know how good she'd had it, that this ice skating instructor was sure to leave her.

Eventually, he got up from his chair and went to the city pound to discover the sweetest, most sad-eyed mutt he'd ever seen. Pepper. His first. Marilyn had never been a dog lover.

It was Kermit after that, "Kermit the dog," then Hoss and Foss who'd been brothers and now, of course, Benny, who was outside carrying his floppy stuffed puppy with absolute solemnity while the night pressed down on the lawn.

The dog was incontinent and nearly blind. His legs shook whenever he stood, and he hadn't climbed the avocado tree in years, but would wait half the day for one to drop. Walt called him over, patted him, said he was a good boy.

He thought about Marilyn and how he hadn't gone after her, how it had somehow seemed at the time that he didn't have the right. And now he was sure that this was exactly what the ice skating instructor was going to say to him at the funeral before he'd been cut off: *Why didn't you try? What kind of man wouldn't try?*

He thought about Linda, her bruises, her underwear, the rapid-fire unpredictability of her emotional states. She must have come to that funeral looking for something—temporary escape or actual help. The moment when the two of them had looked at that row of photographs and agreed how different Marilyn looked after her second marriage seemed now to have meant something more, not just about Marilyn but about themselves. That if she could change her life, then they could theirs. And it occurred to him that what Linda had said about going to that sushi restaurant so often might have been a quiet plea: *Come back. I'll be here waiting. Marilyn is gone. Take care of me.*

A resolution took him then. Walt stood and made the announcement to his old, shaking dog that he was going to do the right thing. Going to return to New York.

WALT HAD PROMISED himself to stay sober, focused,

inconspicuous all through the wait, but he hadn't known it would take this long. Five nights at this same restaurant, and the plan that had seemed something on par with destiny appeared now as childish, desperate, Hollywood nonsense. Linda's comment about coming to the restaurant so often must have been incidental, something to say. So Walt ordered a vodka rocks with his dinner, ordered another when that one was gone, and generally tried to enjoy himself. The vodka was cold and clean. The restaurant had a retractable front that rolled up to let the night in. Early fall and still warm. His table at the threshold of the bright inside.

A Dodgers/Yankees interleague game was playing on the flat-screened TVs that hung in every corner of the room. And toward the end of that second vodka rocks, Walt began to return to his usual friendly self, commenting to all in his vicinity about the game and telling them to do themselves a favor and order the island roll. When the Dodgers put together a double steal, he gave a cheer, causing a man at one of the outside tables nearby to turn around for the replay. "I don't even know if that's baseball," said the man. "Just sneaking."

"I see your point," returned Walt, who loved sports not for their competition but for their camaraderie and who had seen, over the course of his lifetime, thousands of other men's points on the topic of baseball alone. Walt was wearing the same grey, pinstriped suit and orthopedic shoes he'd had on at the funeral, and the other man, the man outside—who had turned away from Walt without so much as a nod—was wearing a suit too, but darker and of a much more costly make.

The game was interrupted by a newscast about Iraq. Something about Sadr city.

The war of Walt's generation had been Vietnam, but his bad knees had gotten him a deferment. He'd been disappointed at first. But later, when his friends started coming home crippled and broken, telling him how lucky he was, the young man saw how naïve this initial feeling had been, and gradually, he adopted another: that when it came to wanting anything so bad you'd be willing to kill another person for it, well, he just didn't understand.

The other man was making a phone call that had gone unanswered. He slapped his phone onto the table with a violence that rattled his glass. He took a drink, picked up the phone, and repeated the process.

Every now and again, he would turn back around to watch a moment of the game, and at some point, Walt managed to introduce himself, to say what he did and where he was from. The man replied that his name was John, that he worked as a skin doctor. And in this way, the two of them established some distant camaraderie.

It must have been a vodka or two later when Walt saw Linda coming toward him across the street in a shapeless gray dress. He stood, offered a smile. But somehow the smile wasn't met; it missed. Linda hadn't seen him and yet was coming closer, twenty, now fifteen feet away. Walt waved and was about to say her name just before she leaned down to give his new acquaintance John a kiss.

Not until after that kiss did she seem to notice Walt standing with his hand still raised and no idea what to do. A nakedness took her face, a wild bewilderment. This man John was her husband. Her abusive husband. Walt jerked himself back into the chair, trained his eyes on the baseball game, and waited for what might happen next.

LINDA APOLOGIZED TO her husband for being late, but received no reply. She repeated the apology several times, her voice sliding from anxious penitence to tired persistence to plain old sarcasm before the couple dropped into a long, hostile silence.

"I called you," John said flatly. Then more silence.

Walt stared into the baseball game without much seeing it. He thought that John probably hadn't noticed him stand to greet Linda, but couldn't be sure. He hated the continuing silence and the uncertainty about what to do. Eventually then, avoiding any glance in the couple's direction, he got up and veered toward the bathroom, surprisingly unsteady on his feet. Those vodkas must have been bigger than he'd thought.

In the bathroom, he fished a business card from his wallet and wrote on the back of it, *Meet me at the hotel. Anytime you can get away.* He thought he might manage to slip it into her purse, but as it turned out, he didn't need to. Linda was waiting in the hall.

"What the fuck are you doing here?" she demanded.

Walt said something about how he'd been coming here nights hoping to run into her and how John's showing up was just a coincidence.

"Okay," she said, "but what are you *doing* here?"

Walt had an answer. He did. It was intricate and lovely, a kind of confession. It was about Marilyn—how he'd never really mourned her leaving or her death. It was about how he'd been wrong to walk out of the funeral with Linda on his arm instead of taking a moment to speak with Marilyn's son. It was about his deferment from Vietnam and all those fifty-nine years of his life, how it seemed his fate to always be lucky, always be light, and that because of this quality, the depth a man should have was absent in him. This, he wanted to say, was what had caused Marilyn to clank the dishes, to leave him. But he understood it now, understood it all somehow through seeing Linda's bruises. Yes, he knew it was strange and awkward to have appeared so suddenly at this restaurant, and he wasn't going to steal her away from her husband, not if she didn't want him to. It was only that he knew how much happier she—how much happier the both of them—could be.

But this answer would have to wait. They only had a moment now. So he slid his card into Linda's hand and said, with some humor, but also, he hoped, with enough determination as to allow no room for misunderstanding, "I'm here to save you."

HE INTENDED TO leave the restaurant then and was just trying to get the check when Robinson Cano made an impressive diving catch, causing John to initiate a conversation about which team had the better second baseman. Then Linda returned and John introduced her. Walt shook her hand, pretending they'd never met.

"Hey, uh, middleman, hey Walt," said John, "why don't you join us?" He was already moving to the chair on his right, directly across from Linda's. "Sit here, so you can watch your team lose," he said.

Walt couldn't think of what to do. He sat. The offered chair was between the man and his wife, Walt's back to the night.

"Looks like we need more drinks," Walt announced. "What would you like, Linda?"

"I don't drink," Linda lied, causing a trill of excitement to run through Walt, a physical awareness of the situation, its spy-thriller verve.

"We didn't like the effect it had on her," John added. He had the face of a horse with bird tendencies, and everything he said sounded like an accusation.

Walt ordered another vodka rocks for himself and John had a whiskey, while Linda stuck to water. The still scoreless baseball game was interrupted by another newscast about Iraq. And, looking for a way to get the conversation started, Walt shared his usual opinion about how he couldn't relate to the motive behind all that killing.

"You married, Walt?" asked John after a moment.

Unsure whether this question was connected to his own comment or an entirely new line of conversation, Walt answered that he had been a long time ago, but that they'd wanted different things.

"Like what?" asked Linda.

"I'm sorry?"

"What different things did you want?"

Walt had said that about his marriage so many times over the years, but no one had yet asked for clarification. "Just . . . different things," he said. "You know."

"No, I don't know unless you tell me," she said, shifting from curiosity to anger all in the space of a single fly ball.

"Cheated on you is my guess," said John, looking toward Linda. "That wife of yours."

Linda, for her part, didn't respond. She returned to silence, and her face went from tight and anxious to neutral, unreadable—eyes on neither one man nor the other, but settling somewhere in the space of night between.

WHEN THE DODGERS executed a suicide squeeze to take a 1-0 lead, John slammed his hand down on the table so hard that his glass fell to the ground and shattered.

Linda excused herself to go to the bathroom. "Again?" John called out after her, his face red from some mix of anger and embarrassment. "*Again?*"

Then a moment later, when the mess was cleaned up and the two men had fresh drinks between them, John said, "She wants to leave me, Walt."

"How do you know?"

"A man knows. A man who's honest with himself does. I could tell by the way she walked away just now." He threw a sloppy, drunk hand in the direction of the bathroom.

"Do you treat her all right?" Walt asked.

The other man blinked and drank, and drank again. Eventually, he spoke. "No."

The two men turned to watch the game.

John's attitude toward Walt changed after that, becoming both friendlier and more boastful. He talked about how beautiful the apartment was where Linda and he lived and about the ten-thousand-dollar stove he'd bought that she never used. Eventually, he asked Walt to come over to the apartment to watch the end of the game. Just across the street, he said with such need in his voice that Walt couldn't find a way to turn him down.

THE TWO MEN sat on a black sectional couch drinking scotch while John talked about the cost of things: the scotch, the couch, the sleek metal table lamp. Walt complimented each item in turn. It was a modern apartment with bare white walls and a total absence of clutter. All so different from the cozy earth tones, fat cushions, and piles of knickknacks at Walt's own house that he couldn't imagine people actually living here.

"Why aren't any of Linda's paintings up?" he asked.

John turned. "How'd you know she painted?"

"She, uh, mentioned it."

"When?"

"I don't remember. She just mentioned it. You were probably watching the game."

That seemed sufficient for John, who turned his attention back to the TV.

Linda had given Walt several alarmed glances when he'd agreed to come over here, but at some point, she'd given up. Now, she was in another room.

It was still 1-0 Dodgers, and the Yankees couldn't get anything done in the bottom of the eighth. John growled at the TV through gritted teeth, "Come on, come on, *come on*. What, do your pussies hurt?"

Walt stayed quiet.

The Dodgers didn't score in the top of the ninth. And leading off at the bottom of the inning, Derek Jeter struck out. Walt could see the hope go out of John. A slack in his body. A different way of drinking.

A moment later he said he was going to the bathroom, leaving Walt alone. He thought over John's prediction that Linda was going to leave and cautioned himself from assuming it meant she would come to him. Still, the liquor and long night pulled him into one of those dreams just at the outside edge of sleep: he was kissing every one of those bruises, entering her gently as she ever had been.

He awoke to a man and woman arguing from somewhere behind him, and it took a moment to establish where he was and who it might be. He heard his name and that word "fucking," shouted, violent. He needed to get up off the couch, to stand, to defend, to explain, but his cell phone rang from an unknown number, and, without, thinking, he answered it. "Hello? Hello . . . ?" he asked. Then something went wrong with the light in the room. It jutted. It angled. There was a crack, and Walt lay on the floor, his business card with the note on the back fluttering down to join him.

John stood overhead, cell phone in one hand and the rod of the metal table lamp in the other. The rod was bloody; its bulb had exploded. Walt wondered what happened to the lampshade. Somehow, it seemed important to find, put back into place.

John swung the rod again.

Walt tried to roll out of the way, but was hit in the stomach. He was so confused, kept mixing up the broken light bulb with his own broken head.

Another interruption to the baseball game, more breaking news from the war.

"You should treat your wife better," Walt gasped. "She deserves . . . ." But he lost the thought when the pain barged in.

His heartbeat throbbed inside his skull. His body was stiffening, and a taste like battery acid spread over his tongue. The business card lay face-up in a glob of blood. *Walt Threw: Middleman.* The blood soaked into the card's clean white. There was so much blood that he couldn't understand himself as its only source. What he did understand was that he'd been absurd to have come here—that he was old, unarmed, and out of shape.

Another blow to the head. The game was back on, and Alex Rodriguez had crushed the ball for a walk-off homerun. They kept using that word. *Crushed.* He *crushed* the ball.

Realities kept trading places, and Walt was having increased difficulty picking the right one out. He thought he was visiting the widower, the ice skating instructor, who was staying at David's house. The young man had insisted, not wanting his father to be alone. Walt and the widower sat together in the cozy basement watching movies about World War II and agreeing that it was comforting to have such a clear idea about who the good guys were, who the bad guys were, and what it was all about. The widower didn't ask why Walt had come or even hint that there needed to be a reason. And it warmed the lonely man to know that Marilyn had been with such a good person all these years. He asked about their lives together, whether she ever brought up that horse, bird, muffin business and if the widower had noticed the way she called things cute. The widower could recall neither, though the two did agree that she'd been quite a woman. And in the end, they forgave each other, the widower for stealing Marilyn and Walt for not trying to get her back.

Then for a moment it seemed to Walt that he *was* the widower, the ice skating instructor, the thief of another man's wife. In the next moment, he was the skin doctor, the man defending his wife, doing whatever he could. Then he was the wife herself, trying to understand this beating as an act of love.

Still, he was not these people. He was only himself. Walt Threw. Down on the floor. It felt important to keep things straight. Honest. Especially right now. You could imagine Marilyn's baby teeth scattered like seeds that would grow baby trees in the atrium, but you had to be careful. Remind yourself it wasn't true. They were more like bones. Twenty little dead things, and he might soon be a dead thing, too.

Linda stood over him watching. Tragic, maybe, but self-possessed, a woman who would not leave her husband, not even if she told herself she wanted to. It was a fantasy. Walt's fantasy. And maybe her own.

John wasn't saying anything. He was crying. The man on the floor felt sorry for him, for all of them now. "I know," he said as the husband raised the metal rod again.

A clang in Walt's brain, a brownout. The power still on but buzzing low. So either he was very focused on the present moment or else had slid away. And all those hundreds of friendships he had back in California appeared now as light affiliations with people who didn't need him. Not even Jack. Not even Daryl. It was only old Benny with his shaking legs, Benny who Walt should have put down months ago if only he'd been able to face it.

What then, if he got lucky? Survived all this? He'd buried so many dogs, and it seemed unlikely he'd be able to muster the optimism required to get another. Then there he would be. There in his house. Sitting in his reclining chair. Wandering alone from room to room, light on as he entered, off as he left.

That next blow hadn't yet arrived. And it began to seem a very long time, so that Walt's waiting sharpened into something else, something more like anticipation. Like ordering one more vodka rocks when he'd had enough already.

KINK

THIS HIDEOUS MAN at the sex shop, this Muppet made of meat, leads me through the stages of a woman's life by way of vibrators.

"These are popular with the sorority girls," he says of the small, pastel lipstick tubes, "Those there are good for women about to get married" of the primary-colored American missiles, straightforward and optimistic. "But when the women get older, they tend to branch off. Bad marriage. Divorce. She'll usually turn to the realistic stuff. Realistic but bigger, understand. The man she thought she was getting. What do you want this for, anyway? What's the purpose of the tool?"

"Christmas," I tell him. "A Christmas gift."

"Yeah, but what's it for? Couple's play? Just for her?"

And what do I say? Do I tell him that back when she was stuck in a safe, unsatisfying marriage, Kate had short-circuited her last vibrator by wiring it to a car battery in hopes it might deliver more? That this new vibrator will be some kind of ironic reference to that story? That I'll be gone a few weeks visiting my parents, and I simultaneously want and do not want to invite her? What I finally settled on saying is "Both."

And he seems to accept the answer. Walks me over to a glass case. "Or else," he says, "they get into kink. Anal beads. Remote control. This one here attaches to your iPod, adjusts along with the rhythm of the music. Or here," he says, picking up a thick, fingerless hand, translucent with ball bearings inside. "This . . . now this is for a woman who knows what she wants." He turns on its motor, invites me to grip the thing, feel the power of its vibration-rotation deluxe.

Then the presentation is over, and it's time to decide. "What are you feeling?" he asks. "What do you want?" His Muppet eyes are the drooping, oval kind, the kind that evoke pity, mine for him, his for me. He waits. He's patient, a sage and Freudian both, knowing the weight of my decision—a question of character and maybe even of fate, because we are our genitals.

When the sex shop man and I were first easing into this conversation, this inquiry into the right vibrator for Kate, he told me a story. A certain woman came into the shop looking for a harness. And then she invited him over to her apartment, where she tied him down and shot a thousand volts into him with a defibulator.

I think there's a moral there, but I'm not sure what. Something about how all men deserve punishment just for being what we are. Something about the close relationship between lust and danger, or the wonders of being tied down.

And maybe if I could answer that question, then I can answer this one, too. What is the right vibrator for Kate? A thirty-five-year old woman who skips a lap around the table when she likes my carrot soup. A silly-serious woman who giggles in her sleep, sneers before orgasm, puzzles out blank verse and contracts for home loans. A woman I can't seem to run away from, despite all my practice and talent for it.

Or to sneak up on this question from its opposite side, which of these vibrators do I most resemble? What corners of pleasure do I nudge in her, and how long can I manage to keep doing it?

This whole thing is starting to seem like a bad idea. Maybe buying a woman a vibrator is just an admission of my inadequacy or my desire to be replaced. Or both. What if it's both—the second because of the first?

The ugly man, the sex shop sage, he's still looking at me, blinking at me like he knows what I'm all about even if I don't know myself.

But I go ahead, get her some approximation of what I figure she'd want: a purple, forked, modern art thing that doesn't look too much like a cock, and so doesn't, I hope, suggest replacement, but addition. It's an *addition*.

Later, I gift wrap the vibrator while thinking about all the things wrong with me: flighty, cerebral, oversexed. On the card, I write my most sincere attempt at confession: *Dear Kate, I'm not the man you think you're getting.*

"Yes, you are," she says when she reads it. "Yes. You are."

A. ROOLETTE? A. ROOLETTE?

ON APRIL 18TH, at the Yarley-Woodward Country Club, we hold our fiftieth reunion. Seventy-three attend, half our original number. "Half," we tell each other, proud of our longevity. "Half," we say, to explain how important our identity as the South Pasadena High School Class of '57 has always been. Waiting at the entrance are nametags that include our senior class photographs. We wear them good-humoredly, chuckling and shaking our heads at those former selves as we might at a kitten pouncing a sock.

The men of '57 are broad in neck and chest and gut, with heads that bulge from buttoned collars like fingertips from tightly wrapped Band-Aids. Our faces, already pink with age, have gone sheepish red as the result of complaints we'd been making only fifteen minutes earlier about coming to this thing— complaints nearly forgotten now as we greet our equally hot-faced friends. We wear navy blue or gray sport coats; our ties are tasteful and subdued, except in the case of Class President Jerry

Riggs, who sports a yellow tie with the word *Viagra* repeated hundreds of times in capitalized blue. And then there is John Mink, a small, chalky man who has just been saying to his young wife in the car that this ought to be a nice event but who now stands apart, ungreeted, running his hands over the jacket of his five-thousand-dollar black tailored suit as if to smooth it beyond what is possible.

The women are not as easily summed up as the men and never have been. Some of us wear black dresses, and others silvery red, some slacks and blouses, others sweaters baggy enough to hide everything except their own weave. Our hair is generally dyed to cover the gray and permed to compensate for the sparseness, but here is Darla Manning braving a clean, otherworldly white, and here Suzanne Straight, hair lush as it was at sixteen. It isn't only her hair that has kept its beauty, but the woman herself. The other women attribute this to posture; "Straight Suzanne Straight," they whisper, echoing the old epithet. But Bill Archer asserts it's because she's been single all this time. "Marriage," he says, not exactly *at* his wife, Caroline, but in her vicinity, "takes years off our lives." The greatest uniformity among the women of '57 is in the ample use of makeup: heavy ruby lipstick and thick powder. But even still, we are far more variously expressive than our men. Compare, for instance, the red avalanche that is Bill Archer's face to the lively alertness in the face of his wife, Caroline. She has just put her hand to the back of Phillip Hughes so that she might say hello, and now, as he turns around, her eyelids widen to let out just a little more blue, then flicker down to let out just a little less. But it isn't Phillip Hughes after all. It is one of the husbands from another school, another class. And now her expression becomes a complex mix of disappointment, embarrassment, and cheery welcome.

In compliment to the senior class photographs on our nametags, photos will be taken this evening too. The set consists of a solid black bench and a sky blue background. Most couples sit side by side, but sometimes the wife sits while the husband stands behind, hands on her shoulders—protectively, valiantly. For those of us arriving alone, the photograph is frightening. Tammy Hitchcock, for instance, works hard on assembling some kind of plausible smile while she squints into the eye of the camera as if into the eye of an old rival she can't quite place. No one says that the black bench looks like a coffin, but seeing Tammy there, we begin to think it. This is the first hitch of the evening, the first reminder of regrets: a trip to Fresno that ended in divorce, a hard-lined stance toward a daughter who now refuses to come to the house, the preschool teacher with the colorful shoes . . .

It is Forsythe Scott who lightens the mood. He wraps one arm around Tammy Hitchcock's waist and the other around Suzanne Straight's, plops onto that black bench with a woman on each knee, and winks into the camera like Hugh Heffner, so that we're all laughing.

THE COUNTRY CLUB is dark wood and forest green, a style we had considered luxurious in the fifties but feels outdated now, "old persony," as Caroline Archer puts it. Round tables draped in white and seating six occupy a room about the size of our high school gym. Half the tables are unused, and that half of the room is left in the dark. The Archers share a table with Suzanne Straight and Forsythe Scott. These four are what is left of a certain crowd. Under the table, Forsythe Scott is digging thumbs into his arthritic knees. His doctor had just warned him not to stress them, and here he has propped a woman on each. Back in high school, he had been so careful, a pessimistic romantic, who, for every hour he would spend imagining sliding an arm around the waist of the lovely Suzanne Straight, would spend three more going over all the ways she would reject him if he did. As a man, too, he has been that way—a buyer of warrantees, a reader of contracts. But ever since the death of his wife two years ago, Forsythe Scott has changed. These days he finds himself taking bold, bounding actions as if in ten-minute fits of drunkenness. The self-doubt only comes later. Yes, he thinks, Suzanne had laughed along with the others when he pulled her onto his lap, but he could feel her tightening and knows what she's like. Even now, she eyes the waiter pouring her wine, stops him at a quarter glass. Forsythe Scott worries and tries to quit worrying. Then he yanks the bottle from the waiter's hand and laughingly pours her glass full.

Two of the chairs at the table are still empty, though it isn't long before John Mink and his wife stand behind them. "I'm sure you don't mind," says John with a false self-assuredness it has taken him decades to learn. "You'd have to ask my wife," returns Bill Archer. "I think she's waiting for someone else." And it's true; she's still waiting for Phillip Hughes to arrive. Aloud, she says to John Mink, "It's only one of Bill's little jokes. Don't listen to him. I never do." The rest of the group smiles, nods, does what it can to make John and his wife feel welcome, the stinginess of fellowship so characteristic of high school having long been replaced by a generous "why not" approach. John introduces his wife to each, throwing their names out one after another with the indifference of a man dropping pennies into a tray of change. Nonetheless, he speaks without having to look at their nametags, while the four are still grabbing glances at his. Each knows the name, recognizes the skinny, near muscle-less boy in the photo, but cannot quite place them exactly—until the thought comes nearly all at once: this is the kid who cried.

Mrs. Mink is twenty years younger than her husband and nice to look at, but somehow mismatched. There is an awkward ratio between slim hips and full chest, and a frequent, jerking readjustment of body that makes her seem not quite up to the brazenness of that low-cut gown. She holds up her martini. "To John's friends," she says, and the group is too polite to correct her.

THE EVENT IS being videotaped for posterity. We are clownish and uncomfortable in front of the camera, feeling pressed to make accounts of ourselves and what we have accomplished in the past fifty years. We mention jobs, offspring, and how long we've been married, but then there is a tendency to trail off. And, certain there must be something left to add, we make jokes or offer silly, cheek-puffing faces. Three drinks in and feeling the camera on him, a class member whose son has been institutionalized because of a schizophrenic breakdown slaps a pat of butter on his forehead, looks around the table, and asks if someone could please pass the butter.

Dinner is roast chicken and steamed vegetables. We don't have the appetite we used to, but Forsythe Scott might just compensate for us all. He sets both arms on the table, encircling his plate as if to ward off potential grabbers, and chomps openmouthed through everything, while Suzanne eyes him in disgust. "It isn't worth it," Caroline Archer is saying. "Three kids, five grandkids. You just worry, is all. As if your heart fell out of your mouth one day and grew into a whole other person. Three people. Eight. Spread all over the country, so when you're done worrying about this one's marriage, you start worrying about the dental surgery of another, and the whole result is that you can't sleep for fifty years."

For Suzanne Straight, it is almost too much to consider that this worried, boasting grandparent had once been Caroline Trill, whose hand used to disappear under the desk to pleasure her lab partner, Caroline Trill who was called the Girl in the Red Velvet Swing after having gone to three different boys' cars during a single drive-in screening of that film, whereas she, Suzanne, had listened to her mother, gone to church, guarded her chastity, and cannot now imagine any good it has done her. Still, the moment passes. Over the years, the disappointment of having waited for a certain kind of man who never came has been replaced by a pride in her virginity, though she sometimes has to remind herself that this self-discipline will only be rewarded in the life to come. "Your first boy is nearly fifty now, isn't he?" Suzanne asks Caroline Archer in order to remind everyone exactly who is innocent and who is not. "Roger, our first, is forty-nine," returns Caroline, simply, cheerfully, as if no scandal had ever existed.

At some point, Caroline mentions a grandson interested in writing screenplays, which gives John Mink an opportunity to tell all that his young wife is a Shakespearean actress at the Glendale playhouse. "Very talented," he says. "It was how we first met. I saw her playing King Lear's daughter, the youngest one, the neglected one. I don't normally go to plays, but a client had tickets. Of course, she's underappreciated in the troupe. The way it always is with talent." Word for word, it is a speech he has given before, and though the speech itself ends in bitterness, though he lowers his head and starts adjusting the lay of a geometric cuff link, one might read on his face something close to satisfaction— not that anyone does. Caroline Archer, for her part, has hardly noticed him speak and continues on with her story. "Bill worries too," she says, "even though he won't admit it. Once our first grandkid came along, Bill was putting rubber on every corner of the house. He spent three thousand dollars on rubber. And now that the grandkids are older, he spends his golden years looking up the safety standards of cars they might drive and the suicide rates at colleges they want to attend."

The group laughs, while Bill Archer answers with the blunt immobility of his hard-set frown. His is a face with a single expression but multiple uses: intimidation, irony, lack of surprise—and what other use might there be? For Bill Archer, there is none.

WHILE DESSERT IS being served, Class President Jerry Riggs takes up the microphone at the front of the room. "We are gathered here tonight," he says in imitation of a wedding, "to celebrate ourselves, our wonderful long-lived selves, who may be getting a little older, a little less effective in certain . . . areas"— here a comic eyeing of his Viagra tie—"but remain brilliant all the same." He raises a glass of wine. "To us," he says, and a toast ripples around the room. Jerry thanks all for coming, then makes some announcements on behalf of those who can't be with us tonight. Mary Robinson, who used to be Mary Freely, welcomes the birth of her first granddaughter, a little late in coming but here all the same. Buck Reilly has recently retired from legal work in Boston and is loving his newfound freedom. Jack and Miriam Pearl say a big "aloha" from Maui and invite any and all '57-ers to come visit their little piece of heaven.

Now a pause. And Class President Jerry Riggs says, "It's never easy to do this part. I thought it would be good idea this time, if, when I call a name, someone could raise a hand to offer a short memory of the deceased. Something nice." Jack Allen's name is called first, and a story is told about the time he borrowed four dollars from the vice principal to bet on a horse through a bookie he knew. When the horse came in first at fifty-to-one odds, Jack kept insisting that he and the vice principal split the winnings. Chris Anderson is named next, and the woman who used to be little Rosie Grech talks about how the two of them used to read *East of Eden* to each other during lunchtime, how this was all their romance had ever consisted of, but how she never could have become a sixth-grade teacher without it. Next it's Joe Bran, whom we all knew as Heavy Duty, and Forsythe Scott tells the famous story of the time Heavy rode his motorcycle off the end of the Balboa Pier.

He had done it for Suzanne Straight, though she is the only one here who remembers that. They had gone on a single date, at the end of which he'd presented her with an entire picture of their lives together. He had money from a dead uncle; they could get a house in Long Beach, start college. Suzanne refused him a second date right then and there. So Heavy spent the dead uncle's money on a motorcycle. Every day after school for three weeks, he would ride up to the front of her house and rev it until her mother came out yelling. Then Heavy would rumble away, while Suzanne looked down from her window feeling something a little more than pity and a little less than love. Then one night, he rode the thing off the end of the pier. At the time, she thought of it as just more proof that he'd been unsuitable all along. She hasn't thought of it often over the years, but every now and again, when a customer at the DMV would call her *lady* without bothering to look at her nametag or face, the memory would barge through.

The names continue: Lacey Cole, Brian Cuddy, Abraham Dale. We find comfort in the heartwarming stories and in the capable leadership of our class president, the optimist with a nickname for nearly every one of us, who, despite what he said, really does make all this seem easy. Only John Mink is irritated, hot inside his suit. He doesn't want to be irritated, not if no one else is, and this makes the irritation all the worse. "Don't see why there has to be such a show," he mutters to his wife. "Oh, John, it's a nice thing to do for them," she whispers back in a light singsong, as if the dead are not dead at all, only lacking the correct change to get on the bus. *She's an idiot*, he thinks. It comes like a twitch, the quick release of a certain muscle usually held tight. "I'll get you another drink," he tells her, eager to get away both from his own angry thoughts and from the roll call of the dead.

The bar is not in a separate room, only in a corner of this one. "Martini," John says to the bartender, "for my wife." The clipped syntax, like the suit, serves to calm internal turmoil and to distance this man from the boy he used to be. The crying had begun during a freshman history filmstrip about Julius and Ethel Rosenberg. John wasn't even aware of it until the film ended, the lights went on, and Frank Hale was pointing at him: "Look, he's crying." And there were the tears, wet on his face. He wanted to explain himself, wanted to say it was something about their way of accepting the death sentence that made him see how people couldn't seem to understand each other, but he didn't know how to say that exactly, which only made him cry even harder, sobbing aloud. For weeks after, they would call him a Jew and a Red until he would start to cry again. Eventually, even those accusations were forgotten, along with his name, and he was only the kid who cried. Now he lays down two twenties for payment and tip on the single drink and carries it back to his wife with the care given to something holy. John rarely drinks himself but experiences the lift of a martini secondhand in the uncomplicated joy that takes over his wife's face as he delivers one to her.

The names continue, and so do the stories. Caroline Archer keeps searching the room as Phillip Hughes's slot approaches. She had understood he would be here, understood he had come to the fortieth reunion and that he lives only fifteen minutes away—that he lives. She keeps recalling the time she and

Phillip had watched the sunset over the Pacific Ocean from the roof of Hoag Hospital when it was still under construction. She wants to get up, move through the crowd searching for him one face at a time. She might have asked Class President Jerry Riggs to see the list of the dead, but then Bill would have made one of his jokes. So Caroline Archer can only sit there listening to a story about how Gary Holnick bowled a 200 and trying to figure out if, between Holnick and Hughes, there are any names left.

Bill Archer, in the meantime, is thinking about the day he agreed to marry his wife. It was the summer after they'd graduated, and he'd had a job moving furniture. She'd come to him on the street, told him she was pregnant. He said he was going to take a walk and would talk to her later. So the eighteen-year-old Bill Archer loped past the neighborhood's squat California houses, each its own bundle of lives, and despite not knowing what to do, he wasn't anxious. It was like moving a great dresser from truck to house, the weight made pleasant by an assurance that he could handle it. At each intersection, he luxuriated in the decision of whether to go left, right, or straight ahead. When, years later, Bill Archer began to suspect that Robert, their first, was not his, it wasn't the betrayal that bothered him most, it wasn't how he had to reexamine the woman he'd married or even how the suspicion threatened to twist the hard, simple love for the boy into something else. Instead, it was the way his suspicion cheapened that day, that walk, that memory. Like his wife, then, but for reasons of his own, Bill Archer listens for Phillip's name. Still, he does so without agitation. He is calm behind his red, stone frown, almost cozy.

The name doesn't come. There are others instead. Sarah Ick. George Jasperson. "Half," says Bill Archer to Caroline. And whatever relief she had at not hearing Phillip's name is replaced with something else. At our fortieth reunion, this list had taken up only a small part of the evening, just as the empty tables had taken up only a small part of the room. Now the list goes on. We can't stop it, and it would hardly be respectful to cut our stories short. So we start embellishing to lighten the mood. Roger Neil is said to have shot five deer in a single hunting expedition. Grace Neckers spent every penny she had on starving children in Kenya, while eating only plain noodles herself. Susan O'Donnell is credited with the invention of the disposable razor. It's a bit shameful, we know, and beneath us; still, it seems to work. We get through Brian Oscar, Jack Paulson, Celia Reserve.

"A. Roolette?" says Jerry Riggs next. "It just says A. I don't know why. Alexander, maybe? Adam? Ashley? Andrew?" He overwhelms the microphone with a sigh. "I'm hoping someone can help me here . . . Who knows this A. Roolette?" He drops his smile. "Does anybody know?" he asks, with a hitch in his voice. We want to help him, to help ourselves. Those in front turn around in their seats, hoping to see a hand go up; those being looked back at turn around too—confusedly, stupidly, since there is nothing back there but the empty tables and the darkened half of the room.

AS SOON AS the dancing begins with "Shake, Rattle and Roll," Harry and Sally Baldwin charge the floor. They have money troubles, probably can't even afford to be here, and yet you wouldn't know it to see their West Coast Swing. He pulls her close, flings her out for a whip, then a left-side pass, while the rest of us look on with approving half-smiles, each thinking in his or her own way that those two are the very best of us. We are not, as a group, death obsessed or youth-obsessed or apt to pine after more than the measure of life given us. When we say we wish to be young again, we mean only that we wish we had our young bodies back and maybe our full sets of choices, but never our entire young selves, so self-doubting and yet so full speed ahead. Still, that unknown name, that A. Roolette, has shaken us, and we are more searching than usual.

"These days there's no restraint at all in the dancing," says Suzanne Straight to Forsythe Scott. "It's just a bunch of sweaty mashing." She speaks with earnestness and a tight, sneaking anxiety. In some ways she speaks for all of us, since it is generally felt that an appreciation of restraint is what we as a generation have to offer the younger set, and the difficulty of having been so little taken up on this feels particularly hard to bear at the moment.

Forsythe Scott nods in vigorous agreement. "Yesh," he says through a bite of cake. A smear of chocolate frosting has somehow gotten onto his glasses.

"Didn't your wife teach you any better than that?" Suzanne Straight asks, and then immediately regrets it. He has stopped mid-chew, his eyes gone soft, so that she sees in them the mild boy who used to drive her to school every day. "I'm sorry," she starts. "I wasn't . . ." she tries. And why, she wonders, are the most reckless men always the most easily hurt? Like her young co-worker, who closed a file drawer on her fingers and then hated her forever after because she'd suggested that if he wouldn't move so quickly such accidents might have been avoided. These silly men, these infuriating men, strutters and grabbers and smearers of frosting, making *her* apologetic, *her* unsure, pressing her into wet, messy places she does not want to go . . . "Your glasses," she says and plucks them off his face, dips a napkin into ice water, and proceeds with a thorough cleaning.

After the first dance, the Baldwins are joined by others— the Pringles, the Housers, both pairs of Johnsons, as well as Forsythe Scott and Suzanne Straight. The lights have been dimmed just enough to soften our edges, smooth us into a crowd. And after several protests, even John Mink allows his young wife to pull him onto the dance floor.

Caroline Archer pulls Bill up, too. Marriage, she tells him, is a compromise, and he responds that it has certainly compromised him. He's a good dancer, though, always has been, and as they move with a sweet, dignified fluency, the thought of Phillip Hughes slides away from them both. But minutes later, there is the face of Phillip Hughes himself only ten feet away, hovering over the white square of a clerical collar. He is not dancing, only standing, smiling, looking—Caroline can't tell— either at the crowd in general or at her. Bill sees the man, too, and stops dancing mid-song. He walks his wife over to Phillip, shakes the man's hand, and announces, from somewhere behind his unreadable face, that he is heading over to the bar. Then he is gone, leaving the two of them alone.

"Just got here," Phillip says. "There was some roadwork. It's good to see you." He is older, of course; we all are. He's acquired a hearing aid and the generous weight of a well-lived life. His smile to her is the same he has just given Bill, the same he has on offer to anyone in the room. She takes his hand, and the two dance. He has no sense of it, keeps wanting to follow the upbeat instead of the down, which gets her giggling. "You better not let me fall, you Phillip!" she shouts. "You better keep an eye on me!" It is the same thing she said to him fifty years ago climbing the skeleton of Hoag Hospital in a loose-fitting skirt and scandalous underwear. Seventy stories up, past where the lift could take them, was a staircase—open and incomplete. Caroline had insisted on going ahead of him, and that's when she had said this about keeping an eye. She knew what she was doing. Caroline Trill was a late bloomer who seemed to burst forth with all the more lushness because she had been held in so long. And the power she suddenly held over high school boys and their fathers, checkout clerks, policemen, even her family doctor was heady and addictive. Yet this one boy, this Phillip Hughes, seemed not to notice; climbing the stairs with his head level to her full and infamous behind, the only desire he expressed was for the sunset. "Hurry up," he kept saying, "or we're going to miss it."

They didn't. The sunset spilled gold all over the ocean, and Caroline Trill scooted in close, determined to see just how far this boy's defenses would go.

THE BAR IS a classic—oak encased in a thick coat of lacquer— and Bill Archer settles into it with satisfaction. The female bartender is a bit big for his taste but young enough to carry it. Youth blazes from her green eyes and the thick, kinky hair could be a living thing in its own right. *Ellen*, her nametag reads, an old-fashioned name. "How many of these things do you do in a year?" Bill asks her.

"'Bout twenty," she tells him. "Are they pretty much the same?" he asks.

"I'd say you've got a pretty spunky group here."

"Well, I appreciate your lying to me."

"Anytime," Ellen says. He orders a Johnny Walker, tall and neat.

In the mirror behind the bar, he catches a glimpse of his wife and Phillip Hughes dancing. It isn't the dancing itself that bothers him so much as the way her imagination must be unspooling some alternate version of her life, a life without squabbles over air-conditioning or whether to put the honey in the cupboard or the refrigerator, a life without insinuations and jabs. But she is forgetting, Bill is sure of it, that there would be other irritations. If not the air, then the coffee. If not insinuations, then honest rage. So maybe it hardly makes a difference, Bill thinks. The choices we make. When we were young it had all felt so important. We had assumed that one date, one night, could determine a life, but the truth is that we'd all get old, all look across a kitchen counter convinced that we deserved better.

Bill feels a hand on his back and turns to recognize Class President Jerry Riggs. "Evening, Bill-o. Not up for dancing?"

"I only ever did it to meet girls," says Bill, "and I guess I got there long since." He has always liked Jerry and orders him a drink.

Ellen the bartender's dark green button-up shirt is not as buttoned up as it might be. And the shift of this shirt, the spills of her hair over those breasts swelling from a white bra could mesmerize Bill all night. He is imagining her nipples, has been told that a woman's nipples are always the same color as her lips, and this woman's lips have a certain shock in their pink. "Are you wearing lipstick?" he asks. "No," she says, but with humor in the smile, referencing, he thinks, what they'd just said about lying.

THE FIRST SLOW dance of the evening is "Put Your Head on My Shoulder," and all the women on the dance floor do, except for Mrs. Mink, who steps back from her husband and spreads her arms out in a slow-motion arc at the perimeters of her reach. She's drunk, John thinks, making a spectacle. "That's not . . ." he says. "Here," reaching to grab those hands out of the air, pull his wife back toward him. "Damnit, John, I don't wanna," she says and starts spinning away. He grabs again. She slips. Her dress flings up; a meaty bare thigh hangs in the air, exposed as she totters for balance, graceless and ugly, jerking the parts of herself back into upright. "I stumbled is all," she says to John, who has a sudden impulse to slap her across the face, but leads her back to the table instead.

Forsythe Scott helps him. He's almost glad for the interruption, the relief from that rocking motion that grinds his arthritic knees. He's never been a good slow dancer, never known what to do with his body, and Suzanne Straight is too stiff to be easily led. Still, he asks her to wait for him, and she does, turning down other offers, so that on returning, he feels himself relieved, indebted. A look passes between them, a naked look that reminds him of the days in his car when she, whose parents wouldn't let her listen to rock music at home, would chirp along to the radio the whole way there. And Forsythe Scott wouldn't need to say anything on those drives, just listen, just smell the peppery sweetness that blew off her skin; it blows off her skin now. And he wants to tell her something, give her something, explain why he is different from how he used to be. "My wife," he says, "was afraid of everything. Sharks, break-ins, freeways. When she got cancer, it was as if she was proud to be right."

Suzanne Straight jerks her head back, intending to chastise him for speaking of his deceased wife that way, but then she sees that his face has gone soft again; he's stuttering some qualification about how he did *love* his wife, it wasn't that . . . And all this somehow bothers Suzanne even more, makes her even more indignant because of the other feelings that come along with it: pity or gratitude, an impulse to make some confession of her own, to apologize for who she has become, to say that her prudishness, like her posture, was a thing instilled so early she'd never had any choice in it, to say that she spends a lot of time watching television alone but never eats in front of it, will not bow to that and so eats alone at the dining room table. Instead she returns her head to his shoulder and makes a humming sound that might signal understanding or even contentment. Instead she softens herself against him—just a little.

Forsythe Scott feels that softening and is touched, bemused; he thinks about the way she had plucked and cleaned his glasses and wants to ask her to marry him. Ask her tonight. Right now. It's a silly thought, he knows, and yet it butts at him hard.

Nearby, Caroline Archer is wondering whether Phillip Hughes can even hear her. His responses keep arriving at odd, approximate angles, so that, for example, when she tells him she's missed him, he says back, "We've got a good thing going over at St. James. Full house. You should come sometime. You and Bill." His slow dance is formal, friendly. And when it ends, he introduces her to an old woman in a daisy-print dress. "My wife," says Phillip Hughes. "Margie."

All at once, Caroline understands that she had pushed that first dance on Phillip and then assumed the second, understands that this woman has been patiently watching the whole time and that she is probably not, in truth, any older than Caroline herself. She has simply given herself over to age more gracefully; she wears no makeup, only kindness, on her face. "Such a pleasure," she tells Caroline. "Phillip says you were a good friend to him back in the days before he met his best." And with a sly, almost mischievous grin, Margie points a finger up at the ceiling, so that Caroline understands that by "his best" she means not herself, but God.

When the young Phillip Hughes sat next to the young Caroline Trill on the roof of the construction sight that would be Hoag Hospital, most of what he did was talk. It was something lifted from Mr. Yarb's science class about how the light breaks up in the ozone to create all those sunset colors. He did not scoot closer to Caroline, did not touch her, and she almost told Phillip that if she wanted to hear all that sciency stuff she would have invited Mr. Yarb up here himself, and he'd have been happy to come too, she knew he would . . . But Phillip was talking with such breathless urgency that interruption was impossible. "It's like," he said, "when Lewis and Clark came here, the whole goal was to get to the ocean, and that's an amazing accomplishment, right, but there's something sad about it too, because it means you've run out of land. But then there's the sunset on the water, which sort of looks like this whole other land, this perfect land that you can walk out onto. So you look at this, this right now and because the journey's over, it's gotta be enough."

At the time Caroline Trill thought this, right now, would be enough if only he'd stop talking and turn his head toward her. But he didn't. He never did. They hadn't even kissed that sunset. And why she went on letting Bill suspect that their son Roger might actually belong to Phillip is a thing she has never explained to herself. It has something to do with the frown that began to settle on his face so soon after their marriage and something to do with the way he just walked away from her on the dance floor without any sign of jealousy. It has to do with needing Bill to believe—needing herself to believe—that she had had choices, while in truth Phillip Hughes was never one of them. On that roof talking of Lewis and Clark, Phillip was everything he ever would be, a lover less of people than of ideas. And maybe she was all she ever would be too—already dating Bill, already four weeks pregnant and sensing it. Still, what she remembers most about that moment on the top of Hoag Hospital, what she has chosen to remember, is not the implicit rejection from Phillip Hughes or the way her life was narrowing so sharply already, but that golden ocean in front of her. That promise of a whole new land.

BACK AT THE bar, Class President Jerry Riggs orders another round for himself, for Bill Archer, and for John Mink, who'd been walking by in pursuit of his wife's coat, wearing a smile like wet cardboard when Jerry Riggs intercepted him. "Minkerbean," Jerry had said, "come have a Scotch." And because his wife was passed out on the table after having embarrassed him, because he was asked so chummily, John Mink did. He could hardly get the first Scotch down but would not betray that in front of these two men. The second went more easily.

Now the men are on the third, raising glasses in a toast. "To young, beautiful bartenders who never gave us the time of day," Bill proposes. "To distinguished gentlemen who never asked for it," returns the young Ellen, raising a glass of her own. Bill wonders if she means it, then decides it doesn't matter. He will take the compliment all the same.

"If she were a bimbo," John Mink is saying of his wife, "but she isn't even a bimbo. And to tell you guys the truth I'm . . . not sure what she is. Even though I married her." He hadn't planned to say all that. It has leaked from him like a long sigh, and like a long sigh it feels good. He drinks down more Scotch, snaps free the top button of his shirt. "I appreciate this, gentlemen," he says, "this drinking with you. I looked up to you in high school, Bill. And so this is appreciated, because," he says, trying to keep focused on the warbling thought. "As you get older, things get . . . I never had children. I could have been that A. Roolette. I almost was. But now I'm not. You just gave me that nickname, Jerry. I haven't had one, except the kid who cried, and that's not a nickname, that's not right. I'm. I'm. I'm Minkerbean."

The truth is that John Mink hasn't cried since high school—not at his wedding, not when his father died. But now, when he says his newly acquired name, the tears come. Quiet tears, but plenty. Tomorrow, he will wake up and hate himself. But for now, at least, it feels like a triumph—the best thing he's ever done.

Class President Jerry Riggs thumps him manfully on the back, and the three sit in silence for a while. Then Jerry asks Ellen, the bartender, "How many of these reunions can there possibly be?"

"I've seen sixtieth."

"How many people were at the sixtieth?"

"Not very many," she says to Jerry, to whom, unlike Bill, she's under no obligation to lie. "

And after that," says Jerry, "there's just no point, is there? You call around, and there's no one left to call."

"Or else," she says, "you don't call around."

"Right," says Jerry and takes a drink. "Because you're dead." He orders another round, proposes another toast. "To what's left," he says.

TWO YEARS FROM now, a heart attack will knock Class President Jerry Riggs off the swim step of a friend's boat, and he will drown. Over time, John Mink's wife will smooth out her awkwardness and come into her own, brash and elegant with lovers rattling behind her like the empty cans we used to tie to wedding cars. And in the half-decade of dementia that will finally result in his death, John will see her alternately as his nurse, his prison guard, and the daughter he never had. The Archers will manage much as they have; she will die first, in Hoag Hospital, and he, romanticizing her far more than he does now while she is living, will follow soon after.

The fifty-fifth will be here at the Yarley-Woodward Country Club, too. There will be no dancing. Our number will be halved again, and more.

The sixtieth reunion will be held in an old tearoom, where pieces of sunlight squeeze through the windows. Seven people is all, none of whom had known one another in high school, none of whom will remember Heavy Duty riding his motorcycle off the Balboa Pier, or the sunset on the water from the top of Hoag Hospital, or who John Mink even was.

213

But some, at least, will remember this, this right now: Out on the dance floor in the middle of "The Monster Mash," the sixty-eight-year-old Forsythe Scott steps back to look the sixty-eight-year-old version of his high school crush full in the face. Then slowly, slowly—shaking in pain, stiffness, and determination—he kneels down onto one arthritic knee.